IT'S A LOVELY WORLD...

He was a reporter. A good one. An average guy with a sense of humor and reasonable views about the rights of his fellow man. Maybe that's why the Monolithians picked him to head up their public-relations program. After all, they had to reach a lot of average people and even though they were invulnerable, they couldn't afford to take chances. Because they had a message, and EVERYBODY had to be convinced. So he didn't have any choice in the matter...

That's where the system went wrong...no choice.

Act peaceful. Love thy neighbor. Obey the law. Why, people could go mad living that way. And many would.

D1572440

CAST OF CHARACTERS

SAM KENT
He thought that he had a great life, then he was abducted by the aliens and found his life had quite a different meaning!

MONOLITHIANS
These aliens wanted to bring peace and prosperity to Earth, at least that's what they said.

EURYDICE PLAYFAIR
Riddie Playfair was not exactly an old war horse, but she wanted the spotlight and got a job right in the thick of things!

IAN MCEACHERN
He knew something was fishy about the way the aliens handled certain things, so he thought he'd find out exactly what…

JOSHUA HOLCOMB
This White House Press Secretary's special talent was keeping everyone in the dark when something was wrong…

PRESIDENT "GOV" ALLISON
All he wanted was to finish out his term and retire to a good life, and this 'alien invasion' business had no place in his plans!

30 DAY WONDER

By
RICHARD WILSON

]

ARMCHAIR FICTION
PO Box 4369, Medford, Oregon 97504

*For more information about Armchair Books and products, visit our
website at...*

www.armchairfiction.com

Or email us at...

armchairfiction@yahoo.com

Yes, an' no, an' mebbe, an' mebbe not.
—Edward Noyes Westcott, David Harum

CHAPTER ONE
(JULY 22, TUES.)

IT WAS an ordinary July morning. July 22nd, to be exact. A Tuesday. Already hot at 8:20 A.M., which is when I got off the long-distance bus at the Port Authority terminal and walked the few blocks to my office in the *Times* Building on 43rd Street.

I work for a wire service called World Wide, and my job is to edit American news and send it to London for relay to clients around the world. Actually, wire service is a misnomer, because we use radioteletype, called RTT. My name is Sam Kent.

I hung up my coat, which I had been carrying, rolled up my sleeves and sat down at the big news desk opposite the overnight editor, Charlie Price. WW operates 24 hours a day.

"Morning, Charlie," I said. "Anything happening?"

"Not a thing."

"Good." I started to read the copies of the news stories, which had been filed to London, since I'd left late the previous afternoon. This is called reading in.

A copy boy automatically brought me a cup of coffee, heavy on the milk, and I lit a cigarette and read the stories on the torn-off yellow teletype paper attached to the clipboard.

At a quarter to nine I was up to date. I got up and took Charlie's place in the slot. "Good night," he said, and went home.

"Morning Nan," I said to Nancy Corelli, the teletype operator. "Ready for a big day?"

"Hi, Sam." She put down the *Daily News* and gestured at the teletype to London. "It's dead as a tomb."

The belt was on. A belt is a length of perforated tape, glued into a circle, which goes through the transmitter and sends on the RTT, over and over, a series of lines that look like this:

QRA QRA DE WFK40 VIA PREWI/NY RYRYRYRY-RYRYRYRYRY

QRA QRA DE WFK40 VIA PREWI/NY RYRYRYRY-RYRYRYRYRY

They're call letters for the radio frequency assigned to WW by the FCC.

The belt had been on for a long time. Ergo, no news.

"Here comes Washington," I said. "They'll change all that."

At my elbow, the direct teletype from our Washington bureau clicked and hummed. It said:

GM NY IM

That would be Ian McEachern, the bureau chief. I said good morning back:

GM WA SK. DEADEST HERE

LOOKS QUIET HERE TOO. MARRINER CANCELED PC BUT ELLS MIGHT HAVE SOMETHING AT THE BRIEFING.

Secretary of State Rupert Marriner usually has a press conference on Tuesday, but today he was getting ready for one of his trips. Ells is George Ellsworth, the State Department spokesman.

II, I told Ian, which is teletype shorthand for aye-aye, or OK.

Having read everything on our file, I pulled over the clipboard with the overseas news. This comes in from WW's London bureau on teletypes at the other side of the room. Our desk doesn't have anything to do with that operation except to react to any major story affecting the United States or the United Nations. The UN machine at my other elbow was still quiet. Normally nothing happens there till after 10.

There wasn't much overseas news, either, despite the fact that London is five hours ahead of New York time.

I went through the papers to see if there was anything Charlie Price had passed up which was worth stealing or following up. *Times, Trib, News, Mirror.* Nothing. *Wall Street Journal.* Damn good reading, as usual, but nothing in it for us. *Journal of Commerce.* Nope. *Morning Telegraph,* the voice of the turf. No overseas angles to the day's quota of horsy news. *Variety* wouldn't be out till tomorrow and the advance copies of *Time* and *Newsweek* would come in later in the morning, about the same time as the first afternoon papers. It looked like one of those days.

The domestic wire service we subscribe to was also in the doldrums. Its ticker had been silent for an hour except for the occasional CLR it sent to show it wasn't dead.

The Canadian Press machine was similarly moribund. I made a tour of the Western Union and cable-company machines at the sides of the newsroom to see if our national stringers or South American correspondents had produced anything the copy boy might have overlooked. Nothing.

"Any coffee?" I said to the boy.

"Heavy on the milk," he acknowledged.

"Thanks."

WW keeps a hot plate in one corner. There's also a kettle, a giant economy size jar of instant coffee, containers of milk from the *Times* Cafeteria upstairs, a five-pound sack of sugar and a dozen or so heavy army-surplus cups. We take our coffee breaks at the desk.

John Hyatt came in about 9:30. He's WW's general news manager.

"Nothing doing at all, John," I said.

"Well," he said, "the situation can't always be fraught." He went into his office off the newsroom.

Nancy Corelli put down the *News* and picked up the *Mirror.* The belt went round and round.

"I'm glad they don't pay us by the word," she said.

"Calm before the storm," I said. "You wait."

"I'm waiting." She turned to Walter Winchell.

I brought the portable radio out of the corner and plugged it in at the desk. Sometimes on a dull day NBC or CBS will dredge up an exclusive of its own, which evokes comment—and a few hundred words of copy—from the White House or the Pentagon.

I heard the tail-end of *Stardust* on the independent station the radio had been tuned to; then, at 10 A.M., switched to NBC, turning down the volume till it had got the horrible electronic gongs with which it heralds its on-the-hour news out of its system.

"...aftermath of a freak tornado in Kansas, and then a special report from Washington on a possible harbinger of the interplanetary age. But first—this message for Anacin..."

I downed the volume again. The interplanetary item might be something, but I wasn't too hopeful. An NBC man could have got the editor of *Missiles and Rockets Magazine* to lift the tarp a bit on a development that was common knowledge in the trade but which Defense was keeping under a secret wrap.

"...and now the news...twister no casualties reported... We switch now to Washington early this morning...Burning Tree Country Club's 16th green...halo of blue flame...alien creatures...completely unsubstantiated but no one has offered an alternate explanation..."

Well! I scribbled a few notes, then got on to our own Washington people on the printer:

IM. NBC RADIO SAYS SPACESHIP MAYBE LANDED BURNING TREE. PEOPLE FROM OTHER PLANET GOT OUT DISAPPEARED AND SECURITY CORDON THROWN AROUND SHIP. SOUNDS FANTASTIC BUT WHO KNOWS. UNTOUCHING PENDING YOUR CHECK. SK

Ian teletyped back:

SK. HAVE A ROUGH NIGHT? IM

WOULDN'T KID U. ASK NBC WA IF U DOUBT.

OK, WIL TRY PENTAGON BUT DOUBT GET ANYTHING BUT HORSELAUGH.

He was back in a few minutes.

SK. MAY BE SOMETHING TO IT. PENTAGON UN-
DENIES BUT UNTALKING EITHER. SUGGEST U PUT
OUT WHAT U HAVE AND WILL TRY BURNING TREE.
IM.

OK

I sent a brief item, thoroughly sourced to NBC and quoting a
Defense Department spokesman as refusing to confirm or deny.
Our domestic wire service had nothing.

Burning Tree hadn't been in the news since the Eisenhower
administration. They might be eager to talk.

I thought about possible sources in New York. There were
the usual crackpot organizations that would comment on
anything. They'd be volunteering their remarks soon enough.
There were a handful of reputable scientists, personal or
business friends, who would be willing to discuss an authentic
report on a non-attribution basis. I decided to wait a bit before
calling one of them.

I didn't have to wait long. The bell of the TWX machine
rang and the copy boy turned it on. He typed WW GA PLS as I
looked over his shoulder. A message began to come in. It was
a queer one. I read it as it came in and then, when the boy had
acknowledged it and torn it off, I took it to the desk and studied
it. It said:

THE MINISTRY OF FOREIGN AFFAIRS OF
MONOLITHIA TODAY TRANSMITTED THE
FOLLOWING NOTE TO THE DEPARTMENT OF STATE
OF THE UNITED STATES: IN THE INTERESTS OF
INTERPLANETARY AMITY THE REPRESENTATIVES
OF THE MINISTRY OF FOREIGN AFFAIRS OF MONO-
LITHIA WHO HAVE THIS DAY EFFECTED A LAND-
FALL ON THE PLANET KNOWN AS EARTH (SOL III)
DESIRE TO CONCLUDE A TREATY OF PEACEFUL
INTERCOURSE WITH THE REPRESENTATIVES OF
THE UNITED STATES AND OTHER TERRESTRIAL
SUZERAINTIES AND TO THAT USEFUL END

SUGGEST A MEETING OF SUCH REPRESENTATIVES AT A TIME AND PLACE MUTUALLY CONVENIENT.

There were several things I could have done. I could have put out a flash saying aliens had landed on Earth. It tended to confirm the NBC report. But my natural skepticism made me pick up the telephone instead. I got the supervisor who handles TWX messages and asked where the message purporting to come from the Monolithian Foreign Ministry had actually been sent from. All the supervisor knew was that it had been sent by BT-107 in Bethesda, Maryland.

"Would that be the number of the Burning Tree Country Club?" I asked her, to nail down a coincidence.

"Yes," she said.

Again I was tempted to send a flash, or at least a snap, but decided to make one more check first. I started to punch out a message to Ian on the teletype to Washington, but that was too slow. I got him on the phone instead.

"I just hung up on Burning Tree," Ian said. "I don't know whether somebody's pulling my leg, but whoever it was claimed to be a spokesman for the Foreign Ministry of something called Monolithia."

"It all fits, Ian," I said, and I told him about the TWX message. "Has there been any indication that State has received such a note?"

"I'll check right now. Hold on."

I bit a pencil while I held on and had a look at the domestic wire service. Nothing there. I wondered what AP and UPI and Reuters were doing. I was sure they had received similar TWX messages. Still holding one phone to my ear, I pulled over another and dialed Plaza 7-1111, AP's number. I put that receiver to my other ear and asked for the general desk.

"This is Kent of World Wide," I said. "Did you get a message on the TWX from something calling itself Monolithia?"

"Yes. Did you? I was just going to check with you about it. UPI and Reuters got it, too. About interplanetary intercourse."

"That's the one. What do you think? Is it a hoax?"

"We don't know. We're checking. Have you put out anything on it yet?"

"No," I told him. "We're trying to get State on it now."

"So're we—"

Ian came in on my other ear: "Sam? State got the note. I'll send a snap."

"Okay," I said and Ian hung up.

"What?" the AP man asked.

"Nothing," I told him. "Thanks." I hung up both phones and turned to watch the snap Ian was sending from Washington. AP and UPI have bulletins. We have snaps. Same thing.

I could tell from the halting way it was being punched out that the regular Washington operator hadn't come in yet and that Ian was sending himself.

SNAP

NOTE

WASHINGTON, JULY 22 (WW)—THE STATE DEPARTMENT TODAY RECEIVED A NOTE FROM MONOLITXXXX A NOTE PURPORTING TO COME FROM A SPACE NATION CALLING ITSELF MONOLITHIA. THE NOTE SAID "REPRESENTATIVES OF…MONOLITHIA" LANDED TODAY ON EARTH AND DESIRED TO SIGN A PEACE TREATY.

MORE

I ripped it off the machine, fixed Ian's correction with pencil, changed "desired" to "wanted," and slapped it on Nan's clip. She had already rung the six bells a snap takes and was up to the dateline by the time she got it.

Ian carried on:

NOTE 2 WASHINGTON ADD SNAP

A STATE DEPARTMENT SPOKESMAN ACKNOWL-EDGED RECEIPT OF THE NOTE BUT DECLINED TO GIVE ANY DETAILS. ASKED IF HE THOUGHT THE NOTE WAS GENUINE, HE DECLINED TO COMMENT BUT SAID A STATEMENT MIGHT BE ISSUED LATER.

RECEIPT OF THE NOTE FOLLOWED REPORTS THAT A SPACE SHIP HAD LANDED AT BURNING TREE COUNTRY CLUB IN SUBURBAN MARYLAND.

A REPORTER WHO TELEPHONED BURNING TREE TO CHECK THE REPORTS WAS UNABLE TO REACH OFFICIALS OF THE CLUB, A FAVORITE GOLFING SITE OF FORMER PRESIDENT EISENHOWER. THE VOICE ANSWERING THE PHONE SAID: "FOREIGN MINISTRY OF MONOLITHIA."

MORE

I sent that straight off to London, then turned to my typewriter to prepare a take to fit into Ian's story.

I typed:

note to washington

first knowledge of the monolithian note came in a message sent by teletype to the major news services. it quoted the note, which it said had been transmitted to the state department. a check with the telephone company, which operates the private line teletype (twx) service disclosed that the message had originated from a teletype machine at burning tree country club.

the message, as received by world wide and other news services, said (full text):

"the ministry...

Ian was sending a message on the machine:

SAM SUGGEST U INSERT COPY OF NOTE WHILE I LOOK OVER MY SHORTHAND ON TALK WITH THIS BURNING TREE CHAP IM

I replied:

ALREADY DOING, and sent my take as NOTE 3.

The direct-line phone from our United Nations bureau rang and I picked it up.

"Hello, Sam?" Collishaw Jones's voice asked. "What's all this about Monolithia?"

"What about it, Collie?" I asked him. "Have you got something, too?"

"It's a handout saying Monolithia is applying for UN membership and requesting the Secretary-General to circulate its petition among all delegates. What the hell is Monolithia?"

I gave Collie a quick fill-in and said, "Put a copy of the handout on the machine, will you? I'll work it into Washington's series. Is there anything in the Charter that says a nation has to be from this planet to be eligible for UN membership?"

"Of course there is—I think. I mean it's never come up before. I'll send the text and then check."

But Collishaw Jones's check showed there was nothing in the Charter prohibiting an alien nation from joining the UN, provided it was peace loving and accepted its obligations.

"There's lots of stuff about international peace and cooperation and international relations," he said. "As far as I can see, the word 'interplanetary' isn't used once. But on the other hand it isn't specifically ruled out."

"Thanks," I said. "That sounds like a good story all by itself."

"I'll do it," he said.

Meanwhile Ian McEachern had sent a few more takes about his conversation with the voice at Burning Tree, which spoke good English in a clicking sort of way, as if it had denture trouble, with an indefinable accent. The conversation had produced few facts, the speaker sticking pretty close to the text of the note, but Ian milked it for as much color as he could extract.

I looked over his copy and handed it to Nancy. I could hear her just busting to ask questions but I didn't give her a chance. I had a thousand of my own and nobody to ask them.

Stew Macon, one of the rewrite men, came on duty and said, "What's new, Sam?"

I handed him the clipboard. "Read this," I said. "Then get Webster and the Oxford and call the library and do a piece on the literal and figurative meanings of 'monolith.' Work in how

Dulles and that crowd used to call Russia a monolithic state, and why."

Stew looked surprised. "Okay," he said. "I don't get it, but okay."

"You will."

Ian was ringing the bell on the Washington machine. FYI. REB, AT WHU, SAYS JOSH JUST CALLED IN BOYS. KEEP U INFORMED.

I acknowledged: II

WHU is old telegraphic code for White House, just as SCOTUS stands for Supreme Court of the United States. Reb Sylvester is our White House correspondent and Josh is Joshua Holcomb, press secretary to President Gouverneur Allison, informally known as Gov.

The phone rang and the operator said, "I have a collect call for anyone at this number from a Miss Eurydice Playfair at Bethesda, Maryland. Will you accept the charges?"

"Oh, God," I said. "Yes, I'll accept them. Riddie? I thought you were on vacation?"

"That you, Sam? I am on vacation but you know how the old fire horse is when it hears the gong. Have I got a story for you, kid!" Riddie Playfair is not exactly an old horse. She's the shapeliest and best-preserved 43-year-old newspaperwoman I know. She combines the enthusiasm of a copy girl just out of college, which is good, with the slangy, wisecracking hyperbole that went out with Lee Tracy's early talkies, which may be why she's still a Miss.

"Well," I asked her, *"have* you got a story for me?"

"Have I? I've got the biggest story since the hogs ate little Willie. Get a load of this, Sammy: I have interviewed a man from a flying saucer!"

"That's fine," I said. "Let me take a snap and you can give the rest to rewrite."

"You mean you believe me?" She sounded disappointed.

"If you're referring to the men from Monolithia," I told her, "they're talking to everybody from State to the UN. But if you saw one, that's news. Go ahead, give me a paragraph."

"All right," she said, crestfallen. "But I more than just saw one. Here goes: 'Bethesda, Maryland, July whatever-the-hell-it-is, doubleyou doubleyou. A reporter for World Wide News Service was kidnapped today by a man who claimed he had come to Earth from a distant planet. Period, paragraph. The seven-foot stranger a few minutes earlier had been seen by the reporter getting out of a huge, circular, wingless craft, which landed on the 16th green at Burning Tree Country Club.' You getting it okay, Sam?"

"Yeah," I said. "That's fine. What were you doing at Burning Tree?"

"I've got friends in high places, and I don't mean the seven-foot stranger. You want this story or don't you? I don't have to work on my vacation, you know."

"Go ahead, Riddie, I'm taking it. You're not hurt, are you?" I tried to sound anxious. "He let you go again?"

"No, I'm not hurt. Will you just take the story?

"'Paragraph. The tall stranger, seeing himself observed, approached the reporter and forced her to go with him'—better make that woman reporter in the lead, Sam, to keep the sexes straight—'to the clubhouse, where he spoke for the first time.'"

"How about some description here, Riddie?"

"I was just getting to it. 'The alien, who said he came from a country called Monolithia on a nameless planet outside our solar system, had a tanned complexion, a prominent nose and long black hair. But except for his single garment, a heavy roughly woven cloak, which covered him from neck to ankles, he could have been taken for an earthman. In some parts of the world even the clothing would not seem odd.' You know what I mean, Sam; fix that up, will you?"

"It's fine," I told her. "I'll get this away and turn you over to Stew for the rest. Give him all the quotes you can and don't worry about the length. You sure you're all right?"

She assured me that she was and I heard her saying "Don't forget my byline" as I passed the phone over to Stew Macon, who pushed his monolithic research aside.

Stew cradled the receiver between ear and shoulder and said, "Okay, shoot, Riddie; give me the gory details. He didn't rape you, did he, honey?" Stew wasn't crazy about Eurydice Playfair either.

I typed out Riddie's story, with byline, and fed it to Nancy a sentence at a time.

Collie Jones had got something meanwhile:

UNITED NATIONS, JULY 22 (WW)—THE UNITED NATIONS SECRETARY GENERAL IN A CAUTIOUSLY WORDED STATEMENT TODAY ACKNOWLEDGED RECEIPT OF THE FIRST MESSAGE TO THE WORLD ORGANIZATION PURPORTING TO COME FROM BEINGS BEYOND THE CONFINES OF EARTH AND ITS IMMEDIATE VICINITY.

THE SECRETARY-GENERAL SAID THE MESSAGE, REQUESTING MEMBERSHIP FOR A NATION CALLING ITSELF MONOLITHIA, WOULD BE CIRCULATED TO ALL DELEGATIONS.

A SPOKESMAN SAID THERE IS NOTHING IN THE UN CHARTER WHICH SPECIFICALLY RULES OUT ADMISSION OF A NATION NOT OF EARTH AND THAT CONCEIVABLY MEMBERSHIP WOULD BE POS-SIBLE. HE POINTED OUT A RECOMMENDATION OF THE SECURITY COUNCIL AND APPROVAL BY THE GENERAL ASSEMBLY ARE NECESSARY TO BRING NEW MEMBERS INTO THE ORGANIZATION...

I sent that, then looked to see if Stew had another take of Riddie's piece ready. He sailed a sheet of copypaper across the desk, grimaced at me and rolled another into his typewriter.

It was all in lower case, wire-service style. Everything comes out in caps on the teletype anyway. It looked like this:

stranger 2 bethesda

in the clubhouse, once the favorite playground of former president eisenhower, the tall stranger said, in good bookish english: "forgive this untypical show of force. i really came in peace, as do my brothers, but i must speak to you lest you misunderstand and falsely alarm the populace."

the reporter got the impression that the man was speaking the truth. "i believe you," she said. the alien smiled, his teeth a striking white against his tan, handsome face.

"ah," he said, "if only we could solve all problems so easily. fervently i hope that our meeting may be a harbinger of interplanetary amity."   more

This was pretty gloppy stuff, I thought, and decided to hold it a while. I caught Stew's eye and he gave a shrug as if to imply that this was none of his doing. Then he said, "What was that? Hello! Hello!" He tapped the little pips in the phone cradle. "Operator, I was cut off… All right, call me back as soon as you can, will you?" He hung up.

"What was all that?" I asked him.

"It sounded like shooting," he said. She stopped dictating and then I heard her yelling. She hollered, 'Don't shoot!' and then there were two shots and the line went dead."

"Somehow I have a feeling it's phony," I said. "How do you feel?"

"I don't know, Sam. I don't think she was acting. Here, have a look."

It was a straightforward description of how the reporter's dictation was broken off and what Stew had heard on the phone. There wasn't much more than he'd told me.

"I don't know," I said. "We'd look pretty sick if it were a hoax. I wonder what AP's doing."

Just then the AC&R machine rang for an acknowledgment and the copy boy brought over a cable from our London office. It said:

21755 THANKS YOUR NOTE SERIES WHICH BIGGEST HERE   RUSH   ALL   POSSIBLE   AMPLIFICATION

AUTHORITATIVE SPECULATION MANINSTREET RE-ACTION ECT

"Okay." I showed the cable to Stew. "They asked for it." I gave Nancy the second take of Riddie Playfair's story to send to London and handed the third back to Stew. "Jazz it up," I said. "If that's the way they want it, that's the way they'll get it. You don't suppose they were shooting at Eurydice, do you? I'll see if Ian can get anything from the Maryland state police. Find out what number she was calling from, will you?"

Stew picked up the phone and I tapped out a note to Washington. Ian acknowledged:

II SHD HV SMTHNG FM WHU IN MIN

Half a minute later Washington gave us this:

SNAP

INTERPLANETARY

WASHINGTON, JULY 22 (WW)—PRESIDENT ALLISON SAID TODAY HE IS "REASONABLY CERTAIN" MEN FROM ANOTHER PLANET HAVE LANDED ON EARTH.

MORE

Good old Nancy had the first part of it in London before Washington finished its sentence.

An informed White Horse souse predicts.
—CBS Washington commentator

CHAPTER TWO
(JULY 23, WED.)

ACTUALLY THERE wasn't much more hard news that first day. I hung around for a while after the night man came on, the way you do when a big story is going, wanting to see what will happen next, but finally I left. I listened to the radio as I drove home from the bus stop, and watched the 15-minute night television news programs, then went to bed.

"Any coffee?" I said to the copy boy as I came in, grinning it in lieu of a good morning.

"You must be the sole support of Brazil," he said.

"Africa," I said. "This powdered stuff comes from Africa."

"It's an education being around you, Sam," he said.

I said good morning to Charlie Price and read in.

There had been, as I suspected, little hard news after President Allison's statement. Much of the night file had consisted of rehashing the known facts and padding these out with interpretation and speculation.

"Washington officials" said the contents of the Monolithian note were being studied and a reply might be expected soon. These would be State Department and White House spokesmen who didn't want to be identified.

"Diplomatic sources" said it was reasonable to assume that Britain, France, Russia and perhaps India and the United Arab Republic had received similar notes. These would be embassy personnel asserting their belief that any sensible aliens would not have snubbed their countries by communicating only with the United States.

"Experienced observers" said receipt of the note had taken officials by surprise and that lights were burning late in government buildings as policymakers tried to cope overnight with the advent of interplanetary relations. These would be newsmen interviewing each other.

"Unconfirmed reports" said any race of people capable of hurtling billions of miles. across space would be sure to have an equally advanced military machine whose weapons would be to our nuclear stuff what our stuff was to the M-l rifle. This would be a roundup of informed guessing and common sense.

I had a look at the late morning papers before relieving Charlie.

The *New York Times* gave it an eight-column headline, three lines deep:

ENVOYS OF SPACE NATION ARRIVE;
NOTE CITES FRIENDSHIP AS GOAL;
ALIENS SEEK U.N. MEMBERSHIP

The *Daily News* said it in four words:

SPACEMEN LAND,
DEMAND PARLEY

"Okay, Charlie," I said, meaning I had read it. "Anything going on now?"

"Washington's not in yet. Jones called from UN a little while ago and said he was working on something. Good night."

"Good night," I said to Charlie. "Morning, Nan," I said to the operator. "Any spacemen out your way?"

"Not yet. But believe me, I made sure the door was locked last night. What happened to Riddie Playfair, anyhow?"

"According to our file last night, she sent a message saying she was all right. Stew Macon followed it up. He'll be in soon. We'll get the inside story."

The UN machine started up:

NILS

UNITED NATIONS, JULY 23 (WW)—THE UNITED NATIONS, FACED WITH THE PROSPECT OF EXPANDING ITSELF FROM AN INTERNATIONAL TO A INTERPLANETARY ORGANIZATION, TODAY CONSIDERED THE POSSIBILITY OF ASKING THE SPACEMEN FROM MONOLITHIA TO MAKE THEIR FIRST

OFFICIAL APPEARANCE AT A SPECIAL GENERAL AS-
SEMBLY MEETING.

NILS NILSEN, THE SECRETARY-GENERAL, WAS
REPORTED DRAFTING AN INVITATION TO THE
LEADERS OF THE ALIEN GROUP SUGGESTING A
MEETING IN HIS 38TH FLOOR OFFICE OF THE SKY-
SCRAPER HEADQUARTERS. INFORMED SOURCES
SAID THAT IF NILSEN THEN WAS CONVINCED OF
THE SINCERITY OF THE SPACEMEN, WHO HAVE
ASKED TO JOIN THE UNITED NATIONS, HE WOULD
CONVENE A SPECIAL ASSEMBLY AT WHICH THE
ALIEN LEADER WOULD PUBLICLY STATE HIS CASE…

Stew Macon came in, saying: "Well, how are all you
inhabitants of the second greatest planet in creation this historic
morning?"

"Keeping the old chin up, Stew," I said. "Say, while you
were grappling with that dictionary piece yesterday, did you ever
find out what the opposite of monolithic is?"

"Come to think of it, no." He grinned. "Paleolithic,
maybe?"

"That'll be enough of that subversive talk. I see by the file
that Riddie Playfair wasn't a casualty. Did you get to talk to her
again?"

"Not exactly. The Maryland cops tried to bust into the
clubhouse at Burning Tree. That's what the shooting was about.
They retired in confusion without anybody getting hurt.
Something about a mysterious defensive shield the aliens have.
The cops got a phone call later. The spacemen said they would
not use force except in self-defense. Then they put Riddie on
for a minute and she said everything was hunky-dory and we'd
be hearing from her again."

"When?" I asked.

"She didn't say. Want me to try to reach her?"

"It's worth a try. Sure."

Stew picked up the phone and I looked over the rest of Collie's UN piece and gave it to Nancy.

Washington clicked in. Ian McEachern told me on the printer that Reb Sylvester had gone directly to Burning Tree in case the spacemen made a personal appearance and that Josh Holcomb had said he might have something later in the morning. He'd had nothing to add to President Allison's "reasonably certain" statement of yesterday. He declined to go beyond that, resisting all attempts to get him to say officially that the aliens had landed.

What he'd actually said, Ian told me off the record, was, "We'll jump off that bridge when we come to it." Asked whether he meant that the United States had doubts about the spacemen's professed peaceful intentions, or that in view of their presumed superior technology the Pentagon was obsolete, Josh had said he'd said all he was going to say.

So much for the White House. The State Department was "studying the situation." The Pentagon sat behind a wall of No Comments.

"No soap on the Alien Friend," Stew said, hanging up the phone. "They don't answer at the clubhouse and the cops say they don't know nothin'."

"We've got to get this story off the ground," I said. "All we've got so far is Collie's UN piece. It's all right, but there's no action. How about calling up the Mayor's office and seeing if they plan a ticker-tape parade?"

"This is action?"

I shrugged. "You got a better idea?"

"I'll call the Mayor's office," Stew said. "Maybe something will occur to me."

I went over to the incoming teletypes to see if WW had developed anything overseas. London's piece was chiefly newspaper comment and unofficial speculation about what the Foreign Office would do. Cooperate with the aliens if they were friendly and resist them if they were not seemed to be about the size of it.

Paris reacted in the spirit of Jules Verne. There was an unofficial report that the travelers of space would be invited to moor their vehicle interplanetary to the Tour Eiffel.

Moscow was keeping mum. No mention of the story had appeared in *Pravda* or *Izvestia,* and Radio Moscow was also ignoring it. The foreign diplomatic corps was agog, but no one seemed to have any idea of what the Kremlin's official attitude would be to a true monolithic state.

The evening papers came up. The Post had interviewed a representative collection of cab drivers, waitresses, etc. Israel Kraft, a Bronx hackie, said the seven-foot aliens could ride in his cab any time if they fit, but they better not try to palm off any funny money on him. The manager of the Mayfair Theater, which was showing "I Was a Teen-Age Necromancer," said all bona fide space aliens would be admitted free. The manager of the Gaiety Delicatessen said he assumed the spacemen had to eat and invited them to his place for the best hot pastrami sandwich in New York. Patrolman Patrick O'Hanlon said he'd leave it to the Commissioner to say how they should be treated, but if they tried jaywalking they'd get a ticket just like anybody else.

The *World-Telegram* had a front-page editorial asking how the aliens had managed to get through our radar without detection. It was not the first time the Defense Department and the Central Intelligence Agency had been caught napping, the *World-Telegram* said. It demanded a Congressional investigation.

The third evening paper, the *Journal-American,* said it was reserving judgment on whether the aliens were as friendly as they professed to be and urged Americans to keep their guard up.

SNAP

WASHINGTON, JULY 23 (WW)—PRESIDENT ALLISON ARRANGED A MEETING FOR THIS MORNING WITH THE ALLEGED ALIENS WHO ARE SEEKING TO CONCLUDE A PEACE TREATY WITH THE UNITED STATES.

MORE

I sent that to London after crossing out the "alleged." I figured if things had gone this far they must be for real.

ALIENS 2 WASHINGTON ADD SNAP

A MOTORCADE OF LIMOUSINES WAS SENT TO BURNING TREE CLUB TO BRING TO THE WHITE HOUSE THE VISITORS WHO SAY THEY REPRESENT THE SPACE NATION OF MONOLITHIA.

JOSHUA HOLCOMB, THE PRESIDENT'S PRESS SECRETARY, SAID REPORTERS WOULD BE BARRED FROM THE MEETING BUT THAT THERE PROBABLY WOULD BE A STATEMENT LATER.

SECRETARY OF STATE RUPERT MARRINER CANCELED HIS PLANNED TRIP TO SOUTH AMERICA TO BE PRESENT AT THE MEETING.

MORE

I asked Ian:

WHAT TIME IS MEETING? ALSO WHOSE BYLINE?

He replied: 11:45. MINE. REB IS WITH MOTORCADE.

I sent that information off as an FYI to London. Ian had little more that was new, but he paged on several paragraphs of background.

John Hyatt, the general news manager, came in from his office. He read the latest and said, "Good stuff. Have you got enough bodies?"

"We're not overstaffed, John, but we're all right for now."

"Okay. We can haul a few people in from Chicago if necessary. And let me know if you need another hand here today. I think I can still bang the old mill."

"Thanks, John."

World Wide has found that if you saturate the field with first-rank outside men you need only two or three men on the desk. Too many bodies have a tendency to get in each other's way.

Reb Sylvester had wangled a limousine with a radiotelephone and was dictating a running story on the short drive from Burning Tree to the White House.

The aliens, about a dozen of them, were wearing the heavy, rough-looking cloaks, which Eurydice Playfair had described yesterday. They were accompanied by more than twice that number of Secret Service men, Maryland state police, State Department security guards and Washington police.

The cavalcade sped along River Road, then into Wisconsin Avenue and through Georgetown. There hadn't been time for many people to hear about it on the radio and few crowds gathered.

But then the cars went past the White House gates without entering. Reb said he couldn't find out what was going on. The cavalcade was headed in the general direction of the National Press Building at 14th and F Streets. That's where we have our Washington bureau, as does almost every other news organization. I could imagine Ian rushing to his window for a glimpse of them.

The cars came to a stop on F Street, strung out in front of the Press Building and the Capitol Theater, where they immediately snarled auto and street-car traffic. The cloaked aliens got out, as did the security men in their neat suits.

It looked as if the aliens were deliberately snubbing the President; as if they intended to keep him waiting while they held a press conference. They couldn't have picked a better place, if that was their intention. There are more reporters per square foot at 14th and F Streets than anywhere else in the world.

But the aliens didn't enter the Press Building. Instead they crossed F Street, which by now was clogged with crowds of curious people ignoring the Don't Walk signs and clustering around the aliens, who politely pushed through them and went into the Young Men's Shop.

They came out twenty minutes later, dressed in neat, conservative suits, which made them indistinguishable from the security men.

They got back into the limousines and circled back the few blocks to the White House, where they arrived on the dot of 11:45 A.M.

"And then what happened?" my wife asked me at supper.

"My God, Mae, you must have heard it on the radio. And they televised the press conference."

"I saw that, Sam. But what's the good of having a husband in the news game if he won't give you an eyewitness account?"

"It's not a game," I told her for the hundredth time. "And you don't get an eyewitness view from the desk."

"You know what I mean," Mae said. "Robert E. Lee Sylvester was there." That's Reb's full name and my wife likes the sound of it. "What did he say? You know, off the record?"

"Not much: The meeting with Gov and Marriner lasted about two hours. Then they all came out and all they said was that they were going over to State. They talked there for another hour or so. Then they came out and posed for pictures and Ells said they'd had a useful exchange of views."

"Who's Ells?"

"George Ellsworth, the State Department spokesman. Josh said just about the same thing in a statement later. That's Joshua Holcomb, the White House man."

"I know him. He gets more publicity than Gov himself.

Doesn't it confuse people to call the President 'Gov'? What do they call the Governor?"

"Washington doesn't have a governor. It's a city, not a state. Honestly, Mae..."

"All right, Sam. I suppose I should know these things. What happened after everybody exchanged views? Did they sign that treaty?"

"Things don't happen that fast. The aliens went to Blair House for the night. They'll have more talks tomorrow morning and in the afternoon they may come up and see Nils."

"Nils Nilsen, the Secretary-General of the UN. I know him."

"Good for you," I said.

"They look like nice boys," Mae said. "They're all so young and handsome. I hope we can get along with them."

"So do we all."

I told them once, I told them twice;
They would not listen to advice…
—Through the Looking Glass

CHAPTER THREE
(JULY 24, THURS.)

THE OVERNIGHT FILE consisted of about 10 percent fact and 90 percent speculation. Sources close to the White House thought that President Allison had been favorably impressed with the Monolithians and that they would issue a joint communiqué today announcing their intention of signing a treaty of friendship in the very near future. Congressional sources said it was likely that the Senate would want to take a long, hard look at such a treaty before it ratified it. There was some talk of a full-scale investigation of the aliens by the Senate Internal Security Committee.

The factual part of the file included a description of the spaceship, which remained under guard at the Burning Tree Club, and interviews with the manager and salesmen of the Young Men's Shop. The size of the ship indicated that it had not made an interstellar voyage by itself; that it was a sort of scout ship or lifeboat from a much bigger craft which presumably was moored somewhere out in space.

The ship at Burning Tree was about as big as our biggest nuclear submarine. It was wingless and cylindrical and its means of propulsion was a mystery.

The people at the Young Men's Shop, honored at having been chosen to outfit the visitors, described them as pleasant, athletically built men whose height ranged from five feet ten to six-feet three. The aliens spoke excellent, almost unaccented English, but had discussed nothing except the clothing they purchased. They had not paid cash but said the bill should go to the Monolithian Embassy, Burning Tree Club, Maryland. The cloaks they changed from were made of wool much softer in texture than it looked. They had taken the cloaks with them after being fitted from the skin out in Earth-style clothing. It was delicately indicated in one of the stories that the aliens had worn nothing under the cloaks and that they seemed to be human in every respect.

The dozen young Monolithians had barely arrived at the White House for the scheduled morning meeting when it was simultaneously announced by Josh Holcomb and at the United Nations that the aliens were flying to New York immediately. President Allison was going with them in his personal plane.

My second cup of coffee got cold while I handled a series of fast-breaking developments. Gov asked for a meeting of the Security Council at which he would propose that Monolithia be admitted to UN membership. If the Council made such a recommendation, Nils Nilsen would convene an extraordinary meeting of the General Assembly for the purpose of voting on Monolithia's application.

A think-piece by Ian McEachern speculated that this was a tidy way of bypassing possible Senate objections to a U.S.— Monolithian treaty. By going directly to the world organization the Monolithians would in effect be signing a treaty of friendship with Earth, avoiding the time-consuming process of negotiating unilaterally with each of the eighty-odd nations in the UN.

Collishaw Jones contributed a few takes of interpretation from his end. While no one was so undiplomatic as to say it aloud, the thought persisted in many a mind at UN Headquarters that the Monolithians might not be as friendly as they seemed. Thus it would be well to vote them into the UN as quickly as possible, legally and morally binding them to the preservation of the peace. If they failed then to uphold the principles of the Charter, no one nation would be in the perhaps hopeless position of trying to repel their aggression. The combined might of the world's armies would be pledged to deter them: to take, in the words of the Charter, "effective collective measures for the prevention and removal of threats to the peace."

Ian departed Gov and the aliens from the White House and Reb arrived them at Washington National Airport. Gov had a brief statement for the newsreel and television cameras; it was a marathon sentence to the effect that he would personally sponsor the Monolithians' application, which he hoped would be acted on with alacrity, reflecting in a concrete way the friendly feeling he was sure the world already had for the interplanetary visitors, who had shown themselves to be genuinely desirous of establishing bonds of comity and of exchanging cultural and scientific information which undoubtedly would be mutually beneficial.

The President declined to answer questions and the aliens courteously but firmly followed suit. The plane then took off for New York.

WW's airport stringer arrived it at LaGuardia, where Gov made much the same statement and the Monolithians maintained their silence. The party then roared off in a siren-screaming motorcade to the Waldorf-Astoria Hotel by way of lower Broadway and City Hall so that the aliens could have a ticker-tape parade and be officially welcomed by the Mayor.

Stew Macon finished taking the stringer's dictation, then wandered around the desk to watch Nancy Corelli send it off to London. He shook his head.

"What's the matter?" I asked him.

"I don't know, exactly," Stew said, *"but this sure isn't the way I thought the interplanetary age would dawn."*

"From the other direction, you mean?"

"No, I don't mean that, though of course it would have been more soothing to the ego to see Earth people pioneer space travel."

"Well, we did get to the Moon," I pointed out.

"Moon-shmoon," Stew said. "Big deal. What I mean is that it's all too pat. Here we have the biggest story since creation and it has about as much kick to it as a punch bowl at the Temperance Society's convention. It's all surrounded with protocol and rigmarole."

"Would you have been happier if they came down shooting?"

"Maybe I would."

"Maybe we'd all be dead."

"Yeah, there's that. But this way there's no drama, no color. First chance they got they even swapped their native costumes for Brooks Brothers suits. Now they look like everybody else. They might as well have come over from France on the Liberte."

"The French have wider lapels," I said.

"Ha ha," he said. "Look, ma, I'm laughing. No, really, I have a hunch there's more to these characters than interplanetary amity or comity, or whatever that old fool Gov called it. I have a feeling they're up to something we're not going to like at all. They're too smooth. Everything's just too smooth."

"Shall I mark your words?"

He shrugged. "File them in the circular file."

"Did you read Collie's piece? He hints at rumblings in the corridors. You're not the only one with a suspicious mind."

"Good for Collie. I didn't see it. Where is it?"

I handed him the clipboard and he went back around the desk.

The phone rang. I answered it: "Desk, Kent."

"Sam, this is Riddie. Want a story that'll stun 'em in the Strand?"

"Where are you?" I asked her.

"I'm at the Waldorf. I've got a suite with three telephones. This is class, man."

"I thought you were a captive of the invader. How did you escape?"

"Escape hell. They hired me. I'm their information officer."

"Their press agent, you mean? I thought you were working for us?"

"I quit; Tell Hyatt my resignation's in the mail."

"Fair enough," I said. "Now we know where we stand. What's your story?"

"I just told you. Earth gal joins aliens."

"Is that all? It might just make a paragraph. How about some real news? Like where they came from and how long they're going to stay?"

"No comment, pal. It's a pleasure to say that for a change instead of hearing it."

"What are they really up to? What are they—explorers? Traders?"

"No comment; no comment. They'll say what they have to say in the Security Council tomorrow."

"Tomorrow? I thought it was going to be today."

"No, tomorrow. This is the pukka gen, laddie. They won't have their speech ready till then. I'm collaborating on it. I'll see that Collie gets an advance text. Maybe even tonight, embargoed for about noon tomorrow."

"Thanks," I said.

"Don't thank me. AP and Reuters and UPI'll all be getting them at the same time. Can't play favorites, you know."

"How much are they paying you?"

"Plenty," Riddie said. "They're loaded, son. If you want to get on the bandwagon I might be able to fix it up for you."

"Thanks, but I'll string along with the poor old Earth types for a while. When are your boys going to hold a press conference?"

"I'll let you know."

I tried to get her to say something story-worthy but she seemed prepared to no-comment me to death.

"I gather that was Eurydice Playfair, girl reporter," Stew said when I hung up.

"Girl press agent," I told him. "She's on their payroll."

"She always was an enterprising old witch. She give you anything?"

"Only that the Security Council meeting's been postponed to tomorrow, she says. Will you ask Collie about that? I want to tell John Hyatt he's just lost a staffer."

Collie checked and confirmed that the meeting had been put off and gave us a story to that effect.

Soon afterward the Gov-alien cavalcade reached the Waldorf and holed up for the night. Reb Sylvester, who had been assigned to the Presidential party, gave us the word that the lid was on, meaning that Josh had told the press there'd be no more news today. Gov was putting the finishing touches to his speech and the Monolithians were preparing theirs.

It was turning out to be the dullest big story of the century.

"Mark my words," Stew reminded me.

"Which ones?" I asked him. "That it's a complete bust, or that it's going to erupt?"

Stew merely grinned.

Fortunately for the file, a good torso murder turned up in a coin locker at Grand Central and that occupied us until it was time for me to go catch my bus.

> We come from a world where we have known
> incredible standards of excellence...
> —Thornton Wilder

CHAPTER FOUR
(JULY 25, FRI.)

PRESIDENT ALLISON, the dozen aliens, and their entourage rolled smoothly down to United Nations headquarters in their limousines and were whizzed up to the 38th-floor skyscraper office of Nils Nilsen.

They ignored a ramshackle group of writers who were picketing in UN Plaza. Two of the writers wore beards and all of them looked self-conscious. One of the placards they carried said: SCIENCE FICTION WRITERS' GUILD—ALIENS UNFAIR TO SCIENCE FICTION. Another said: SPACEMEN GO HOME; YOU'RE RUINING OUR RACKET. A handful of sub-teenagers, clutching copies of *Galaxy* and *Fantasy & Science Fiction,* gave them an occasional cheer and occasionally a new arrival sought an autograph. The UN police looked on tolerantly. One of them said: "Poor guys. First sputniks. Then Moon rockets. Now this."

The President, the Secretary-General and the aliens, each of whom had picked up a dispatch case to go with his Earth-style suit, came down the elevator and went to the Security Council chamber.

The Council was called to order. Allison read his speech proposing membership for Monolithia. The chief delegate of the space nation was invited to address the Council. He read his speech, five hundred words of platitudes, which didn't deviate by a comma from the advance copy Eurydice Playfair had delivered to the wire service overnight.

The Council voted unanimously, 11 to 0, to recommend that Monolithia be admitted. The Council adjourned and Nils Nilsen called the General Assembly into extraordinary session for that afternoon. The Assembly met at 3 P.M., unanimously voted Monolithia in, then adjourned until its regular September session.

The UN thus became an interplanetary organization, with Monolithia pledged to uphold its peaceful humanitarian aims.

It had been an easy story for the desk to handle and we had it all wrapped up before my relief came in.

Then Riddie called and said the aliens had scheduled their first press conference for 6 P.M. in her suite at the Waldorf. I asked John Hyatt if he wanted me to cover it.

"I don't think you need bother, Sam," he said. "The reinforcements from Chicago arrived this morning. We'll send Red Melville and a couple of his juniors to help Reb. They haven't had a big story since the Chicago fire."

"Okay, John. I'd as soon watch it on television."

As I was driving home from the end of the bus line I heard on the car radio that Congress had voted to give the Monolithians the freedom of the United States. The Senate, reassured by the aliens' acceptance of the principles of the UN, had originated the bill and the House immediately shouted it through. The President signed it on his return from New York, saying it gave him great pleasure inasmuch as it granted the visitors from space all the rights and privileges of U.S. citizenship.

Mae fixed us an armchair buffet and we ate while we watched the press conference on TV.

There was the usual milling around at the start. I saw Reb Sylvester, putting in overtime, and Red Melville and a few other reporters I recognized from the wire services and papers. Eurydice Playfair and two of the aliens sat at a table on which was a cluster of microphones. An announcer for the television network was describing what we were seeing and giving us background information we already knew.

"I see your friend Eurydice is doing all right for herself," Mae said, full of those overtones a wife has for any female in the office who is under sixty.

"Mmm," I said. "She quit us. Shh."

The television announcer made some introductory remarks, then Riddie made some and introduced one of the aliens (who were wearing their Young Men's suits) as Mr. Reev. She spelled the name.

"Are there any questions?" she asked, and there was a roar of laughter as dozens of hands shot up.

Reev, smiling, indicated the AP man, who asked where exactly Monolithia was.

Reev began an involved answer, which Riddie interrupted, saying a fact sheet containing technical data would be distributed after the press conference.

The UPI man asked what Reev's exact title was. "Permanent representative to the United Nations from Monolithia," he replied.

WW's Reb Sylvester, apparently referring to Stew Macon's piece on the definition of monolithic, noted that this referred to any massive homogeneous whole, such as a state or an organization. "Is there any significance to this term," he asked, "which as you know has been applied in the past to the government of the Soviet Union?"

"We have no connection with the Soviet Union," Reev said, "except those we have established with it and more than eighty other countries through the United Nations." He added with a smile: "As your definitions note, we are homogenized, like your milk."

Amid laughter, Reb asked: "Would you describe your government as a democratic one?"

"Utterly," Reev said. There was no trace of accent in his speech. The clicking Ian McEachern had noticed in the voice of the Monolithian he had spoken to on the phone at Burning Tree was entirely absent, as if they had perfected their study of English.

A Canadian Pressman noted that "reeve" is a term his country uses for the president of a village or town council, and asked if there was any significance in the fact that Reev's name was almost identical. Reev looked baffled, but Riddie said it was merely coincidence. The CP man then asked the name of the other Monolithian.

"Jain," he said, spelling it. He added with a smile: "No significance; it's just a name."

A man from Reuters asked if the Monolithians were aware that President Allison had signed a bill making them honorary citizens of the United States.

"We are grateful for that," Reev said. "But I think you will find that the new law bestows full, not honorary, citizenship."

"Are you prepared to live up to the laws of the United States?" an unidentified reporter asked.

"Fully," Reev replied. "And to those of the United Nations. Not only to the letter but to the spirit of the law."

"Do you believe those laws to be fair?"

"The Constitution of the United States and the Charter of the United Nations appear to be the most perfect examples of humanitarian principles we have encountered anywhere in our travels," Reev said. Jain nodded agreement.

"How many of you are there?" an NBC man asked.

"Twelve of us here in New York," Reev said. "An equal number at Burning Tree. Then, of course, there are hundreds of us in each of the mother ships."

"The mother ships? What are they?"

"The craft which actually made the interstellar journey. They are moored, as some of your press accounts have indicated, outside your atmosphere."

"How far out?"

"As far out as the Moon, but exactly opposite it, on the other side of the Earth."

"Is that why we had no warning of your approach from the observatory on the Moon?"

"Probably. That's the way we planned it."

"Are those ships armed?"

"All our craft are armed, but only with defensive weapons. We travel only in peace and molest only those who would molest us."

There was a stir among the reporters, and a man from *Missiles and Rockets Magazine* asked for a description of the weapons.

"I am afraid that is what you would term classified information. Our representatives and those of your Defense Department and the United Nations Secretariat have scheduled a meeting to discuss possible exchange of information touching on these weapons—which I emphasize are strictly defensive in nature."

"Are you armed personally?" the AP man asked.

"We do not carry concealed weapons, if that's what you mean," Reev said. "But we are capable of defending ourselves against any attack on ourselves or our friends. I don't wish to sound ungrateful, but the elaborate security guard provided for us and your President when he traveled with us was quite superfluous."

"I don't suppose," one of the television men said, "you'd be willing to give us a demonstration of your defense weapon? It'd make quite a graphic picture for the television audience."

"We'd be glad to," Reev said, "if you could suggest a way."

"Well," the TV man said, looking around the room, "I could throw one of these big, glass Waldorf ashtrays at you..."

"Now wait a minute," one of the other reporters said. "We don't want glass shrapnel flying around the room."

"No one will be hurt," Reev said. "You will see. I suggest you focus one of your cameras here." He indicated a spot about two feet in front of his face.

"Okay," the TV man said. He picked up the ashtray, which was a good eight inches in diameter, and hefted it.

"Empty the cigarette butts first, at least," someone said.

The TV man asked Reev: "Ready?"

"Ready."

The TV man let fly. The heavy ashtray sailed directly at Reev's face. About a foot from it, the ashtray appeared to hit, or sink into, an invisible shield. It did not shatter, but seemed to fuse, increasing its diameter but decreasing its thickness. It became the size of a pizza platter, but exceedingly thin. It continued to grow in diameter, becoming fainter and fainter. Then it disappeared completely.

When the hubbub of amazed comment had subsided Reev smiled and said: "Nobody hurt, I trust?"

One of the reporters in the first row said, "No, but I'd swear it's quite a bit hotter up here."

"True. That usually happens when matter is changed into energy."

"Can you be more explicit?"

"Sorry, no."

"Would you have the same protection against a bullet?"

"Entirely the same."

"How much warning do you need to put it into effect?"

"None. It takes effect at the first sight of danger."

"Would it work against a bomb?"

"Yes."

"A hydrogen bomb?"

"Yes."

"Then you're invulnerable."

"Completely."

"Well," a reporter said, "I'm awfully glad you're on our side."

A ripple of nervous laughter went through the crowded room.

It's too hot in New York or else it's too
cold. But hot or cold—somebody's always
pushing you.
—Joe Frisco

CHAPTER FIVE
(JULY 26, SAT.)

SATURDAY was my day off and Mae and I drove into New
York. We had tickets to a matinee. I switched on the car radio.

"Get some music," Mae said.

"I want to see what's on the news."

"Can't you ever relax?"

"I'm relaxed. I don't have to do anything except listen."

"Promise me you won't go into the office," Mae said. "I
want to see that play."

"I have no intention of going to the office," I said. "Not
unless there's an earthshaker."

"That's what I mean. Let somebody else handle it for a
change. You're not the only man who can do the job."

"Listen," I said. "Here's something."

A commentator on one of the independent stations was
saying the Monolithians apparently had made a number of secret
agreements with the United States and the United Nations. The
American public was being kept in the dark about many things
they had a right to know. It was obvious from the alien's press
conference yesterday that they were being more frank with the
public than the people's own government officials. The
defense-weapon demonstration to the nation on television was
only one example.

I recognized the voice, which continued on a note of agita-
tion:

"Here is a bulletin just handed to me. A Monolithian
spokesman disclosed today that the first two-dozen aliens who
landed on Earth have been joined by at least two hundred—I
repeat, at least two hundred—more.

"This disclosure was made in answer to a question, reinforcing this commentator's belief that our own government is keeping us in the dark about matters of which we have every right to know the true facts."

"As opposed to the false facts?" I muttered, my copyreader's instincts affronted.

"Shh," Mae said. "Listen!"

"The Monolithians, on the other hand, appear to be willing to answer almost any nonscientific question put to them, giving at least the appearance of candor which our own officials so sadly lack," the commentator went on.

"The question then arises whether it would be truer to say that our government is *allied* with the aliens, as our officials claim, or whether it is *collaborating* with them, having capitulated to their unknown military strength in a sort of interplanetary Munich."

Mae gasped.

"Clearly it is the aliens who are acting with confidence, publicizing their movements, while the U.S. government shows a curious unwillingness to keep its own people—you and me—informed. Can it be that the government itself is in the dark about these vitally important matters? Can it be that our own government is acting as the tool of the aliens, having secretly surrendered to a power the like of which this Earth has never known?"

Mae had been listening in mounting alarm. "Do you think he's right?" she asked me. "Is it possible?"

"That's old Clyde Fitchburn, the noted viewer with alarm," I told her. "Don't take him, too seriously."

"He can't be making it all up," she said. "Can he?"

"Only about 99 percent of it," I said. "He still hasn't got back to his one little true fact—that two hundred more aliens have landed."

I switched to another station.

"...playing host today to nearly ten times as many aliens as originally landed on Earth," an announcer on one of the network stations was saying.

"Now listen," I said to Mae. "This is news, not an editorial."

"A Monolithian spokesman said the new arrivals—two hundred of them, all male—had landed in a second scout ship, at about midnight, in Central Park, at the northern end of the reservoir.

"The spokesman said in a statement, quote, 'The second contingent arrived in response to the invitation implicit in the law signed yesterday giving the Monolithians U.S. citizenship.' Unquote.

"At nine o'clock this morning, when the stores opened, the Monolithians arrived in a fleet of taxicabs in the midtown area, where they went in separate groups to the different men's clothing stores—Bond, Howard, Ripley, Rogers Peet and Brooks Brothers—and to the men's departments of such department stores as Stern's, Gimbels and Macy's. Here they outfitted themselves in Earth-style clothing, which they charged to the Monolithian Embassy, and left by foot, mingling with the crowds on the sidewalk.

"Dressed like typical New Yorkers, most of them virtually disappeared—that is, they lost their identity as aliens and became indistinguishable from the average male New Yorker.

"The Monolithian spokesman said in answer to a question that their purpose was that of any visitor to New York—to see the sights of the city and become acquainted with its customs."

"There," I said to Mae. "That doesn't sound quite as bad as Fire-Eater Fitchburn's account, does it?"

My wife seemed relieved, but she wouldn't admit it. "They're probably playing it down," she said.

The newscaster said, "Reporters were late on the scene, but if eye witness accounts of passersby are to be believed, the aliens split up into groups of two or three and visited such places as Woolworth's, book stores, movie houses, the Empire State

Building, the Planetarium, and took rides on buses and subways."

Mae said, "I'm not sure I'd like it if one of them sat next to us at the play."

"How would you tell?" I asked her.

"I'd know," she said. "Somehow. I'm sure I would."

"Well," I said, "you let me know and we'll interview him at intermission."

We crossed the George Washington Bridge, went down the West Side Highway and found a place to park on Sixth Avenue in the upper thirties. We had half an hour before curtain time and I asked Mae if she would like a drink.

"I think I would," she said. "I seem to have a slight case of the jitters."

We found a quiet place about a block from the theater and sat at the bar in the air-conditioned dimness. I had a Scotch and soda and Mae had a gin and tonic.

"Had any aliens for customers?" I asked the bartender as I paid for the drinks.

"Not so's I noticed," he said. "At least nobody tried to charge it to the Monolithian Embassy. We got a strictly cash trade here."

He went to serve another customer and a well-dressed young man came in and sat down on the vacant stool next to Mae.

"Sam," she whispered, nudging me.

"What?"

"Here's one."

"Where?"

"Right next to me," she whispered. "Look at his clothes. They're brand new."

The bartender went to the new arrival and said, "What'll it be?"

"What do you have?" Mae's neighbor asked.

"Anything you want," the bartender said. "Whiskey, bourbon, Scotch, gin, vodka. Soda, ginger ale, Seven-up. The combinations are limitless."

"I'll have a Scotch and Seven-Up," the stranger said.

The bartender didn't blink an eye. "Yes, sir," he said, and proceeded to blend the two strange ingredients.

"Scotch and Seven-Up!" Mae said to me. "He must be one of them. Who ever heard of such a thing?"

"That's pretty circumstantial evidence," I said.

"Change seats with me, Sam," she said. "I'm getting nervous again."

"Okay," I said. "Want another drink?"

"Definitely." She swallowed the rest of her first one as she slid onto my stool.

"Two more of the same," I told the bartender.

"Coming up," he said. "Right after this Scotch and Seven-Up." He gave me a shrug.

"Say something to him," Mae whispered, meaning my new neighbor at the bar.

"Like what? Shall I ask him what he thinks of American women?"

"You're the newsman," she said. "You ought to know what to ask him."

"This is my day off," I reminded her.

"Go on. Ask him."

"Okay."

I waited till his concoction had been served to him, then said: "Pretty good drink, Scotch—and Seven-Up."

He looked at me in what seemed to be embarrassment. "I don't know, really," he said. "First time I ever had it."

"Stranger in town?"

"Yes, as a matter of fact. Got in only last night."

"Where from?"

"You wouldn't have heard of the place," he said.

("See! I told you!" Mae whispered.)

"I don't know," I said. "I've heard of lots of places: Medicine Hat, Ephrata, Chestnut Bend, Gallipolis, Moses Lake, Lackawack…"

"None of those," he said, as if he were playing a quiz game. "It's a little place in Missouri called Joplin."

"That's easy.   I got my Signal Corps training near there during the war."

"You don't say!"

("Ask him where he got the new suit," Mae persisted.)

"Where'd you get the new suit?" I asked him.

"Bond's," he said.   "You know, under the waterfall in Times Square? It looked so cool." They have an artificial waterfall on top of the building. It used to be Pepsi-Cola's.

("Ask him what time," Mae said.)

"What time?"

"About nine o'clock," he said. "When it opened. Why?"

("Why?" I asked Mae.)

("Ask him if he saw the aliens in there then")

"Did you see the aliens in there then?"

"I saw a bunch of men come in in bearskins or something like," he said. "I thought it was an advertising stunt."

("He thought it was an advertising stunt," I told Mae.)

("Doesn't he listen to the radio?" she asked.)

"Don't you listen to the radio?" I asked him.

"The radio?"

"The aliens from Monolithia were getting outfitted in Bond's at nine A.M., according to the radio," I told him without benefit of Mae.

"Is that who they were? Well, well."

He drank his Scotch and Seven-Up at one gulp, making a face over it, and said, "I've got to get going. I have a ticket for a show at 2:30."

("What show?" Mae asked.)

"What show?" I asked him.

He mentioned the new Rodgers & Hammerstein musical. "I'm meeting my wife there. Would you like to see a picture of her and the kids?" He took out his wallet to show me.   In addition to the snapshot I saw his Missouri driver's license and an old draft card.

"Nice-looking family," I said.

"Thanks. Got to run now. My wife has the other ticket and I'm meeting her at the seats. Can't get lost that way, I figure. Pleasure talking to you. You, too, ma'am."

He left and I said to Mae: "Well?"

"Well what?"

"Are you satisfied he's not an alien?"

"I don't know. How come he's wearing his new suit the same day he bought it? You always have to wait a week or ten days for alterations."

"Maybe he didn't need any alterations and they cuffed the pants while he waited. At least he won't be sitting next to you in the theater."

"How did he get tickets to that? Are you sure you couldn't do any better than the revival of *Where's Charley?*"

"Not on short notice. He probably paid scalper's prices on the expense account. We'd better start."

We left the bar.

"I guess he won't be," Mae said, backing up the conversation in the way she has. "But for my nerves' sake there'd better not be another man in a new suit sitting next to me, even if he has got a good explanation."

"The odds are against it," I said as we stood at the corner of 44th Street and Broadway and waited at the Don't Walk sign. "Just divide two hundred into several million."

The *Walk* sign flashed on. We were in a group of about fifteen law-abiding pedestrians who started across the street. We had almost reached the other side when somebody yelled, "Look out!"

A big long convertible with a grinning idiot behind the wheel was not only failing to yield the right of way to pedestrians but was making an illegal right turn onto Broadway from the cross street.

I grabbed Mae and hauled her ahead to the curb. "Damn fool!" I hollered at the driver, who kept on going, blowing his horn.

Everybody scrambled to safety except one young man who hadn't seen or heard, or else had supreme faith in his rights as a pedestrian. The convertible was heading straight at him.

"He'll get hit!" somebody yelled. A traffic cop blew his whistle. A woman screamed. Mae, unable to look, buried her face in my shoulder. The pedestrian never broke his casual stride.

The massive chromed bumper was only inches from him when it began to disintegrate.

First the bumper, then the grille and the oversized fender, then the right front tire dissolved in a shimmering film.

As the tire disappeared, the momentum of the car sent it ahead into what was obviously the protective shield surrounding one of the aliens.

More of the car vanished and it came to a grinding stop, its underside providing the brake as it plowed into the asphalt.

The front of the car, almost clear back to the windshield, simply wasn't there any more. The driver's idiot grin had changed to a look of unbelieving dismay as he stared at the nothingness where his hood used to be.

The young man, who I now saw was wearing a new suit, stepped onto the curb near Mae and me. He paused, looked back for just a moment at the remains of the convertible, and said, as if quoting, "A driver must yield the right of way to a pedestrian crossing with a *Walk* signal," then lost himself in the crowd.

ALIEN, n. An American sovereign in
his probationary state.
—Ambrose Bierce

CHAPTER SIX
(JULY 27, SUN.)

IT'S PRETTY COMPLICATED to explain why a person who lives in New York State, as I do, has to go through New Jersey to get home from his office in New York City. It has to do with (1) the way New York's border slopes northwest from the city and (2) a straight line being the shortest distance between two points. People who half-grasp these phenomena remain convinced that my village, High Tor, N.Y., is a short drive from any old place in New Jersey.

John Hyatt, demon respecter of facts though he ordinarily is, was one of those so deluded when he called me on the telephone on Sunday morning and asked me if I'd mind taking a run over to Middle Valley, N.J.

"I'm aware it's your day off, Sam," John said, "but this is practically on your doorstep and I know you'd feel hurt if we didn't ask you to cover it personally."

This, of course, was the well-known malarkey, but I told him, "I'm the original busman, John, but maybe you'd better fill me in. Just what is going on in Middle Valley, of all places?"

"It's these damn aliens, Sam. Incidentally, I want to thank you for phoning in that eyewitnesser yesterday on the jaywalker. I hear you missed the first act of the play on account of it, but it was a damn fine story and we appreciate it."

It had been a jaydriver, not a jaywalker, but I didn't correct him. "Think nothing of it, John. It'll all show up on my overtime slip."

He laughed. Not without pain, it seemed to me. World Wide is in a perennial economy drive and the word *overtime* is not one you use lightly in the business office. "We never boggle where a good story is concerned," John said. "You know that.

And this Middle Valley thing—well, you're aware, I'm sure, that they've got this local blue law banning Sunday employment…"

Middle Valley, N.J., is a good hour's drive from High Tor, N.Y. It's less than twenty minutes via the Lincoln Tunnel from New York City, but I knew John would think I was being uncooperative if I mentioned it. I didn't argue with him. I told Mae I was on overtime, got in the Volkswagen and went.

New Jersey passed a law some years ago aimed at forcing Sunday closing on a group of merchants who sold used cars and major appliances in a string of roadside stores along well-traveled Route 17, which runs between New York City and the Catskill Mountain resorts. The idea was to protect the community merchant from this competition so he could have a day off. But the legislation was too broad and bogged down in courts. Its opponents charged, among other things, that it was discriminatory. What about the Jewish merchant, they asked, who religiously closed his place of business on Saturday, his Sabbath? Was he to be penalized by having to close on two days a week, while the Christian merchant closed only on one?

While the state law was being appealed, its opponents obtained an injunction and Sunday business continued. Some communities who had liked the state law during the brief time it was being enforced then passed local ordinances. Middle Valley was one such community with its own Sunday closing law.

Middle Valley is a residential, fairly well-to-do, predominantly Christian village of about 3,000 people. It has few stores, most of its residents doing their shopping in nearby towns. It does, however have a drug store, a delicatessen, a gas station, a newsstand and a local milkman. The village fathers decreed that the strict law meant all these must close on Sunday.

No one objected except the druggist, the delicatessen owner (who had closed on Saturday for years), the newsdealer and the milkman. The citizens of Middle Valley found it not too inconvenient to order extra milk on Saturday to tide them over the weekend, and they rather enjoyed driving a couple of miles to pick up the Sunday papers. It was a mark of distinction to live in the village that permitted no paid Sunday employment.

"Middle Valley's shut up tighter'n a drum today," the well-to-do, car-owning, Christian citizen could remark with pride as he paid for his paper across the village line.

The few who didn't own cars had to walk as far as two miles to catch the buses whose drivers were not allowed to stop in Middle Valley. No one asked them if they enjoyed their walks, especially on rainy Sundays.

Some of this I knew and some John Hyatt filled me in on. I learned a lot more after I got there, first having checked my gas to be sure I wouldn't be marooned there till Monday.

I parked near the center of town, in front of the delicatessen. Down the block were the newsdealer's, the drug store and a couple of real estate—and—insurance offices. All were closed.

I introduced myself to the man standing in front of the delicatessen. He told me his name:

"Simon Dorfman. This is my store. I closed it Friday at sundown. Religious reasons. I can't open today. Monkey business reasons. I'm thinking of opening today regardless. I'm considering it this minute. But I'm also considering ninety days in jail and $200 fine."

"Who would arrest you if you opened?" I asked him.

"Who? The cops. Who else?"

"Middle Valley police?"

"Joe Lyman and Fred Moffat. I've known them since they were boys. But they'd arrest me. They said so. It's not their fault."

"Then who would arrest them?" I asked Dorfman.

"What do you mean arrest them?"

"Aren't they paid employees? If you can't work on Sunday, how can they?"

He thought that over. "What's sauce for the goose, eh?"

"Why not?"

"But you're a reporter. You don't care if I get arrested as long as you get a story. Maybe I'll talk it over with my friend Hirsch the druggist."

"Let me know what you decide, Mr. Dorfman," I said. "I'll be around."

"Good. But listen. You want a real story? Go down two blocks that way and one to your left."

"What's there?"

"The Middle Valley Congregational Church. I don't want you to think I'm laughing at somebody else's religion, because I don't do that, but go down and see for yourself. Those men are there—from the spaceship. An interesting situation."

So that's where they were. I left him saying to himself, "Sauce for the gander. Why not?"

John Hyatt had said some Monolithians were in Middle Valley but he didn't know why. He imagined they were sightseeing and he obviously hoped for something better. I was beginning to have the same hunch he must have had.

There was a crowd of about a hundred outside the Congregational Church. Most of the people appeared to be parishioners—well-dressed, upper-middle-class men and women. Their late-model cars were parked along the tree-shaded street. I squeezed my Volkswagen in among them.

A separate group of well-dressed people—all young men—stood outside the main entrance of the ivy-covered stone church. The minister was with them, talking heatedly. I made my way through gaps in the crowd of parishioners, who seemed anxious for some settlement to be reached but unwilling to become involved.

"...blasphemy," the minister was saying. His name, according to the outside bulletin board, was the Rev. James Lonsway Marchell.

"Not at all, Mr. Marchell," one of the young men said. "It's merely a question of law."

"God's law has called my flock to worship. Man's law shall not keep them from their devotions."

"Certainly not," the young man said. He was speaking fluent, unaccented English. "We have no quarrel with their wish to honor their deity in whatever way they choose. But you, Mr. Marchell, as a paid employee of this church, may not, under law, work on Sunday."

"Work!" the minister exclaimed. "It is the Lord's work I do!"

"But for a salary paid by men. You have admitted that to be a fact."

"By what right—" the minister said—"by what abrogation of authority do you come from millions of miles away to interfere in the affairs of this quiet, respectable, law-abiding village?"

"The very fact, sir, that you have chosen not to abide by the law has brought us here," the leader of the Monolithian group said. "We have solemnly sworn to uphold the laws of this country, and therefore the laws of each of its parts. We should be shirking our obligations to our adopted nation if we did less."

"You pervert the law—you mock it. You are heretics. Worse, you are the devil's henchmen. I have tried long enough to reason with you. Now stand aside. Again I tell you—I mean to enter my church!"

The minister started for the door but one of the Monolithians was there ahead of him. I was half-afraid I was going to see Marchell start to disappear, but obviously the aliens had a variation on their protective weapon. The minister wanted to enter his church, not to harm anyone, and the shield took the form of a pliant, invisible wall that prevented Marchell from even hurting himself as he walked into it, apparently for the second time at least.

He was bounced back, staggering. Regaining his balance, he turned to address his parishioners:

"My friends, I have done all I can. I shall go now to my study and in solitude pray for guidance. These—creatures—I cannot call them men—have said you may worship as you choose. I invite those of you who wish to do so to enter this house of God and pray..."

The Monolithian at the door stood aside but fewer than a dozen of the congregation went in.

I considered talking to the Monolithians, but decided I'd better file a story first on what I had. I figured there'd be time to talk to them later. It looked like a long and memorable Sunday for Middle Valley.

I drove off to look for a telephone, hoping the village used the dial system and didn't depend on an illegal paid operator.

I found an outdoor telephone booth at the closed gas station. A young man was lounging next to it. He stepped in front of me as I reached to push open the door.

"I'm sorry," he said.

"You must be one of the aliens," I said, though from his appearance he could have been anyone.

"A U.S. Monolithian citizen, at your service," he said, smiling but continuing to bar my way. "Tate is my name."

"Kent's mine," I said. "I'm with World Wide. Just let me phone in my story, then I'd like to talk to you."

"I know who you are," he said. "But you may not telephone. It's the law."

"Look," I said, "it's ten to one Middle Valley doesn't have a telephone office. The call will go through Newark or someplace. Nobody in Middle Valley would be doing anything illegal."

"No," he said, "but you would."

"Oh, come on!" I was shocked. "I don't live here. I'm just a New York reporter. I work for an international news organization. You must have heard of freedom of the press!"

Tate smiled and shook his head. "Mr. Kent, the law may be stupid but it is explicit. No paid employment of any kind is permitted in Middle Valley."

"Sure, sure," I said. "But what's it to you? This will be publicity for you. That's what you want, isn't it?"

"You misunderstand our motives, Mr. Kent. We are your good interplanetary neighbors, repaying your hospitality by observing all your laws, as we are sure you would if you were to visit our country."

"What you're really trying to do," I told him, "is to reduce us to absurdity."

"Don't put words in my mouth, Mr. Kent. Remember when you do dictate your story—and I believe the village border is a mere half-mile away—remember that you said that, not I."

"Half a mile? Come with me, will you? How did you know who I was?"

"I'll join you gladly. Mr. Dorfman told me about you."

He climbed into the car and I phoned the desk from a drug store in the neighboring community of Valley Center, N.J. The store was doing a thriving business in Sunday papers, ice-cream sodas, hot coffee, cigarettes and other typical druggist's goods.

I gave John Hyatt his story heavy on the quotes, the way he likes them, adding a bit about my own encounter with the Monolithian. He made me spin it out at length for a sidebar. I didn't tell him Tate was standing just outside the booth, listening to every word. I was afraid John would have interviewed the hell out of him, keeping me hanging around all day.

I came out of the booth, perspiring from its closeness.

"How about a coke?" I asked Tate. "We won't get one back in Middle Valley."

"Good idea," he said. We sat at a table and a waitress took our order.

"That a Bond suit?" I asked the alien. "Two pair of pants?"

"Simon Ackerman," he said, smiling. "One pair."

"Then you're not one of the original dozen from Burning Tree."

"No. I'm one of the Central Park unit."

"How do you like it here? What do you think of Earthwomen?" I figured I might as well get it asked and over with.

"Very tempting," Tate said. "Remember, we've been a long time enroute."

"How long?"

"Three years."

The cokes came, in tall glasses, heavily iced, with straws.

"What would you do to a vending machine that sold an illegal coke?" I asked Tate.

"I beg your pardon?"

"Never mind. I'm glad you didn't put the whammy on me back there at the gas station. I saw what your pal did to that convertible in Times Square."

"Did you?" He beamed. "Quite an example, wasn't it? It was a pleasure to uphold that law."

"Rough on the car, but the idiot had it coming. Do you mean you're not enjoying what you're doing in Middle Valley?"

"There are degrees," he said, taking a sip of his coke. "It was a pity Mr. Marchell was prevented from holding his service. We are not antireligious, as he asserted in the heat of his anger."

"He was prevented by your people," I reminded him.

"By our people upholding local law," he insisted.

I decided he wasn't quibbling, and said, "Let's get back to where you came from. You said you were three years on the way. Did you know where you were going when you started?"

"Oh, yes. Earth. Sol's third planet. You invited us in 1945."

"Invited you?"

"So to speak. That was Earth's Atomic Year One, you will recall."

"You mean you detected the first explosion?"

"We detect them all. You were the fourth known planet to achieve that level of development. We believe we were the second, in Monolithia."

"The second?" I asked. "Did the people from the first one visit you?"

"The first planet failed to see the potentialities for evil. It destroyed itself. When we had achieved space travel we visited its remains. It was a graphic example to us. We determined then that human life was too rare a commodity to be squandered."

"You think we're too infantile to prevent our own destruction?"

"We think you need guidance. We got it second-hand from Planet I. We were too late to help Planet III. You're IV."

"You mean Planet III destroyed itself, too?"

"So to speak. It's a dead world. Planets II and IV—Monolithia and Earth—are the only advanced worlds left. It's our duty to preserve them."

"What do you mean 'so to speak?' " I asked him. "What do you mean 'advanced?' " I was making full notes and Tate had been watching me fill page after page of copy paper.

He finished his coke. "I've said enough for now." He sounded adamant, and to keep him from drying up entirely I switched the subject slightly:

"How come you speak such good English?"

"English, Japanese, Monolithian, Tildonian (that was one of Planet III's languages)—they're all human tongues. It's merely a matter of adaptation. We don't click any more, you notice. That's a Monolithian trait, but easily de-emphasized."

I scribbled away and he watched me tolerantly, sucking on a piece of ice.

"You know I'm going to quote you. How shall I describe you? As a Monolithian spokesman?"

"If you like. We're all spokesmen. We have—to use a diplomatic phrase, but an accurate one—an identity of views on this urgent matter. Shall we go?"

I sensed that he had dried up.

"I'd pay for the cokes," he said, "but it seems too small an amount to charge to the Monolithian Embassy."

I dropped two dimes at the cashier's counter.

We heard sirens as I drove back into Middle Valley. Smoke was climbing into the sky. I traced it to a burning house and parked a block away. Tate and I ran to the edge of the crowd watching the fire.

"It's the Waddell house," somebody said. It was a big house probably worth about fifty thousand. The smoke was billowing out of a room at the back.

"Who's Waddell?" I asked.

Tate knew. "He's president of the village council. As a matter of fact, he's chiefly responsible for the Sunday closing law."

"That's great," I said, making notes again. "What a story! And now his house is going to burn down because it's against the law to put the fire out. What's his first name?"

"Everett."

A fire engine screamed around a corner and men jumped from it, trailing a hose behind them. Other equipment followed. Within a minute the hose was attached to a hydrant and water was pouring on the fire.

"Hey!" I said to Tate. "What's the idea? Why aren't you stopping them? They're working in Middle Valley on Sunday, aren't they? Aren't they paid employees just like the minister and me?"

"No," the alien said. "Unfortunately for your story and your fine sense of irony, these are not paid employees. They're volunteer firemen."

Never speak loudly to one another
unless the house is on fire.
—Harold William Thompson

CHAPTER SEVEN
(JULY 28, MON.)

I'D GOT HOME pretty late, but the alarm clock went off at six, as usual, on Monday morning. It's at this time of day that I envy my city-dwelling brothers who can get up an hour later and reach their offices at the same time I do. Mae and I had bought a house in High Tor in preparation for the baby, who was scheduled to be born in late November. ("Beautiful timing," our tax accountant once said, thinking of the exemption, which would be good for the entire year.)

I rescued the dew-soaked New York *Times* from the lawn. Its main headline, across four columns, said:

ALIENS KEEP PREACHER FROM PULPIT,
CITING VILLAGE'S SUNDAY WORK BAN

The radio newscasts were hitting it hard, too. I listened to them as I brewed a pot of coffee.

Mae shuffled into the kitchen, sleepy-eyed, in her housecoat. "Why didn't you wake me up?" she asked.

"You have to sleep for two now," I told her.

"Nonsense," she said, giving me a kiss and looking at the front page. "What do you want for breakfast?"

"Eggs, sunny-side up, covered with Pep." You break the yolk and the Pep absorbs it.

"We don't have any Pep. How about corn flakes?"

"They're too big," I said. "You know that."

"I'm sure I'll never learn the fine points of these little mealtime foibles of yours. You want bread under the eggs then?"

"Obviously," I said. It's not obvious at all, of course, but Mae is very teasable.

"Honestly, Sam," she said as she buttered the frying pan, "you could let a little yolk run on the plate. I don't mind washing it off. You're not a bachelor any more, you know."

"I know that very well," I said. It isn't the washing so much as the waste that bothers me. I think occasionally of the tons of dried egg yolks being scraped into the garbage every morning and it gives my frugal soul the willies. "How's Junior today?"

"He's very happy. Not a peep out of her." Mae changes its sex with every reference to keep an open mind on the subject. She even occasionally refers to it in the plural just in case. "You don't think our children are going to suffer from these aliens, do you? I mean they're not going to have to live in oppression under the heel of the invader, are they?"

"Where did you get *that*, for God's sake?"

"On the radio last night before you came home. It was that Clyde Witchburn. You know."

"Clyde Fitchburn. Don't listen to him. Listen to Ed Murrow or Eric Sevareid. Listen to me. But don't let that doom-shouter Fitchburn give you nightmares. It's not good for Junior."

"All right, Sam. You like the aliens, don't you?"

"I like the few I've met personally, but that doesn't mean I approve of everything they do or are capable of doing. I don't think they plan to grind us under the heel, though."

"Well, they're up to something. They didn't come all this way just to obey a lot of funny laws and get people's dander's up. We must have something they want."

"Maybe we've got something they don't want," I said.

"Why would they land here, then?"

"To keep us from exporting it, now that we're on our way to the stars."

"Like what? Germs?"

"Sort of. Uncontrolled radiation, maybe."

Mae slid the eggs from the pan onto the two pieces of bread on my plate. She poured coffee for each of us and said, "Eat, now. It's six-thirty."

So it was. I was out of the house in ten minutes. I bought a *Herald Tribune* before I got on the bus, leaving the *Times* for Mae. The Trib had a righteous editorial headed "Abuse of Hospitality." I skimmed through it. It said about what you might expect. Lippmann wasn't in the paper that day and Alsop was discussing something else.

I folded the paper and wriggled around in the seat. Buses are like candy bars, I thought. The price goes up and the size goes down. Each new bus seemed to have less legroom and a lower headrest than its predecessor, so that you had to be a contortionist to take a nap.

I had found a reasonably comfortable position when two men got on, took the seats behind me and continued a discussion they'd been having about the aliens.

"I told Alice they'd better not fool around with the church in our town."

"Damn right."

"I said you can go so far, but some things you just don't fool around with."

"You said it."

"I told her, 'Alice,' I said, 'you mark my words, just let them try in Old Corners what they did in Middle Valley and there'll be trouble.'"

"What did she say?"

"She agreed a hundred per cent, of course. Now I'm not a fellow who goes every week—you know; but Easter, maybe Palm Sunday, and Christmas—but by God some things are sacred.

"I tell you I got so mad when I saw that on the television. If that's the way things can happen, I told Alice, I said, 'Listen, if this is what they expect us to put up with, believe me, they've got another thing coming.' You don't just take something like that sitting down."

"I should say not. Why, I said the same thing to—"

"I mean there's a limit. I don't pay much attention to what goes on at the UN—I don't suppose anybody does—but when it gets as close as this, I tell you, things have come to a pretty pass, my friend, a pretty pass indeed."

"They sure have. I told Virginia—"

"I'll bet you did. It's a crying shame when a bunch of fancy Dans from Lord knows where can walk in on us and try to upset the things we hold sacred..."

This stimulating conversation must have put me to sleep because the next thing I knew somebody was tapping me on the shoulder and saying, "Last stop, Mac."

I said thanks and got out.

A bar on Eighth Avenue had a new banner up over its door. "Welcome Monolithans," it said. My copyreader's eye noted the misspelling. Nobody inside looked fancy enough to be one of the alien Dans.

The teletypes were clattering away at World Wide. The summer doldrums were sure over.

"Morning, Sam," the copy boy said. "How about some coffee?"

"Morning, Herb," I said. "That's the first intelligent remark I've heard in some time."

"Heavy on the milk?"

"That's right—Earth-style."

Charlie Price was pecking away at the typewriter. "Morning, Charlie. What's doing?"

"Somebody called up from an outfit called the Society for the Prevention of Alien Domination of Earth. Ever hear of it?"

"No, but the initials spell 'spade.' Are you sure it wasn't some bright P.R.O. for a playing-card company?"

"Never thought of that, but it could be. There's something in it about digging in and holding the line. I'll finish it and leave it for you."

"Good." Herb brought my coffee and I sat down to read the file.

"John Hyatt's in already," Charlie said.

"Already? He was on the desk yesterday, too. He must be alien-happy."

"How'd you make out in Middle Valley? I saw you got a byline."

"Well, I didn't get a chance to put any expense money in the collection plate," I said.

Charlie didn't answer that and I wondered if I'd offended him. I went back to reading the file.

I had barely taken over from Charlie when John Hyatt came into the newsroom. "Hi, Sam," he said. "I've been on the phone with Riddie. She was about as informative as an AEC handout, but I gather something's up. I'll take the desk again today. The Chicago crowd'll be in soon to help here. I'd like you and Stew to shoot up to the Waldorf. I don't know what's cooking but I suspect the aliens may be in a flap over their shenanigans yesterday. Nice story, incidentally. It got splashed all over Europe, according to the play report."

"Good. And thanks for the byline."

"You deserved it. Sometimes I wonder why we're wasting you on the desk."

"I like the regular hours," I said.

"Well, it looks as if regular hours are going to be out the window for the duration."

"Where is Stew?"

"He'll be in at nine. You make a good team, you and Stew. I've noticed that. I'd like you to keep as much of an eye on Riddie as on the Monolithians, if you can. I suspect that little gal knows a lot more about what's going on than she pretends. Get her off in a corner and pump her, if you can."

"Shall I bring flowers?"

I meant it sarcastically, but John said, "She's not the bouquet type, but Head Office has authorized extraordinary expenses for this story. The sky's the limit. Make love to her, if you can stand it, but find out what the hell is cooking."

Nancy Corelli had been all ears. "You never authorized him to make love to me on the expense account," she told John. "We could have had some high old times."

"I'm shocked, Nan," said John, who hadn't been shocked since he climbed a high-tension pole as a kid in ought-eight. "You're a married woman."

"Sam's married, too, don't forget," Nancy said. "And here you are egging him on to go to bed with that old broad."

"Just a figure of speech, Mrs. Corelli. Suppose you let us old trench coat boys cover the story and you concentrate on sending it to London."

Nancy accepted the rebuke in her own fashion. "I'm glad I have an honest job, at least," she said.

Stew Macon, came in. "I see by the daily press there have been a number of developments since I left the shop last Friday," he said to John and me. "Good morning, Nancy."

"Don't talk to them, Stew," Nancy said. "They'll corrupt you, the old lechers."

"Now what's this all about?" Stew asked.

"Tell you in the taxi," I said. "Don't take your coat off. We're on detached service."

"Good enough. But I hope you have a big cash reserve, Sam. I happen to have spent—and I use the term advisedly—a very expensive weekend."

"Keep in touch," John said. "There are two of you, so let's have a phone call every so often even if nothing's doing."

I filled Stew in as the cab driver wended us uptown.

"I wasn't kidding about being broke, Sam. This little babe I met had very expensive tastes."

"I'm good for about thirty bucks," I said. "Then I'll have to get a refill from petty cash."

"There's nothing petty about cash," Stew said.

Eurydice Playfair's suite was crowded to its expensive walls with reporters, State Department people, Pentagon people—including some high brass in uniform—and waiters. A bar was set up along one wall.

"At this hour of the morning?" I asked her.

"It's there for them as wants it," Riddie said. She was drinking coffee herself.

There didn't seem to be any Monolithians present yet, but then no one could tell for sure. I asked Riddie.

"No," she said. "We're saving them for the floor show."

"Something big?"

"I didn't lay on this spread just to say hello."

"Do they know what's going to happen?" I said, meaning the U.S.A. contingent from Washington.

"No, they're just liaison. But, believe me, they're fairly perishing to know."

"Whatever it is, will it make them gasp in the Ginza?" I asked.

"Sam," she said, "this'll pierce them in the Place Pigalle."

"Ah," I said, "but will it crush them in the Kremlin?"

"I have no more to say right now. Why don't you have some coffee?"

"I think I'll have a weak little Scotch and soda, if it's all the same to you."

"It's not the same as coffee, that's for sure."

A man from the Journal-American took her away and I went to the bar. Stew was already there with a glass of something that was neither small nor weak.

"Did you pump her, Sam?" he asked.

"She's a dry well."

"I have circumnavigated the room and there is nothing. Sealed are the lips. Or blank are the minds, I don't know which."

"You sound as if you've been talking to the man from *Time*. Give John a call, will you, Stew? He might want a little color story."

"He always wants a little color story." He went off to one of the two-dozen telephones Riddie had provided.

I asked the barman to weaken up my drink with more soda. Caterers are always very generous with the customer's whiskey.

Riddie got up on a chair at the end of the room and clapped her hands.

"I guess everybody's here," she said. "I've asked you to come here this morning, ladies and gentlemen, to meet two other members of the ambassadorial staff from Monolithia. They will enter through this door on my right in a moment. Before they do, you may wish to make a note of their names. They are Mr. Quy—spelled Q-u-y but pronounced "Key"—and Mr. Brown."

Stew, back from the telephone, whispered, "Have you noticed how all of them have one-syllable names?"

I nodded as I wrote them down.

Somebody asked Riddie, "Would it be correct to assume that these gentlemen hold a higher position in the Monolithian government than the ones we've previously met?"

"Not at all," Riddie said. "Everyone in Monolithia is equal. Each has the rank of Ambassador."

"But," the questioner persisted, "maybe these new ones intend to apologize for the incidents of yesterday in Middle Valley."

"Certainly not," Riddie said. "The Ambassadors who visited Middle Valley acted in complete accordance with the law. There is not the slightest doubt in any Monolithian mind on that score."

"So much for John Hyatt's hunch," I muttered.

Stew spoke up. "Would you say, Riddie, that there was complete and unanimous support for the Middle Valley delegation among the Monolithians?"

"Yes, I would. To them, laws were made to be obeyed."

"How about the groundswell of protest..." somebody else started to ask, but Riddie raised her hands.

"Please," she said. "What happened yesterday has no connection with this meeting. In fact, I think you'll have a bigger story today if you'll just let me get on with it. I'll now ask the Ambassadors I've named to step into the room."

The door opened. The two men came in. They were dressed in the same conservative style as their predecessors. But their faces were different. Mr. Quy was an Oriental. Mr. Brown was a Negro.

I'd dictated my story and turned the phone over to Stew to elaborate on it. Riddie came over carrying two drinks. She handed one to me. "It's not weak this time," she said. "I figured you could use it."

"Thanks," I said, taking a good swallow.

"Well, Sam," she said. "Is this a story or isn't it? Do you think it'll fracture them in France?"

"Baby," I told her, "you're too far out. This will lay them low in Little Rock!"

Scientists have reached general agreement in
recognizing that mankind is one: that all men
belong to the same species, Homo sapiens.
—UNESCO Statement on Race, 1950

CHAPTER EIGHT
(JULY 29. TUES.)

WE'D ALREADY had the highlights of the Mount Pelley
story from the local wire service but it had left a number of
questions unanswered. I looked in the stringer book to see who
we had in Mississippi. To my surprise I found that we had a Mr.
Elbert Patterson right in Mount Pelley. I sent him a wire asking
for at least a thousand words, with good color and quotes. His
story was on my desk in less than two hours. Here it is:

Mount Pelley, Miss., July 29 – The bus driver said, "Move to
the back of the bus." When the Negro passenger failed to obey,
the driver shouted at him: "That's a white man's seat you're in,
nigger. Get back where you belong or I'll throw you off."

The Negro, a neatly dressed man of about thirty, carrying a
briefcase, replied quietly, "This is an interstate bus. Under
Federal law I have a right to sit where I please."

Eleven other passengers were on the bus, which was due to
pass through this town on its way to Biloxi. Six were whites.
The other five Negroes sat without objection in the rear section,
traditionally reserved in this state for "colored."

The Negro man who refused to move was sitting alone in a
double seat three rows back from the door. He turned and
looked out the window.

His attitude infuriated the driver, Merle Cagle, who pulled
the bus to the side of the road, slammed on the brakes and
strode down the aisle.

"I'll give you one last chance, black boy," Cagle said. "Move
back or get off."

There is confusion among the other passengers who reported this conversation today as to whether the Negro replied, "Don't touch me" or "You'll be sorry."

A great deal of confusion surrounds the ensuing incidents. The bus driver claimed the Negro passenger hit him with both fists and kicked him. The white passengers said the Negro man hit the bus driver with his briefcase, which they presumed contained something heavy, using it like a club. The Negro passengers said the lone Negro man sat still, making no effort to defend himself.

Whatever happened, Cagle was severely cut and bruised on his hands. In addition, the big toe of his right foot was broken, a hospital report said late today.

Cagle went back to the driver's seat and brought the bus here. He parked it in front of the office of Sheriff Ellis Grout, whose name became nationally known several years ago in connection with the fatal beating of a 13-year-old Negro boy who was said to have "sassed" a white woman. Grout had refused to arrest or question the two white men who boasted that they had administered the fatal beating, saying they were just big-mouths "trying to take credit" for the crime.

Grout, an admitted Kleagle in the Ku Klux Klan and a leader in the local White Citizens movement, was sitting in front of his office in a chair tipped back against the wall when the bus stopped.

Cagle jumped out and pointed to the Negro man sitting at the front of the bus. "I got somebody for your jail, Sheriff," Cagle said.

Grout asked a few questions, then said through the bus window: "You must be one of them northern niggers. Well, this ain't the north, so suppose you just come out of that bus."

When the Negro passenger gave no sign that he had heard, Grout went into the bus, drawing his pistol.

"I gave you an order, nigger," he said. "Get your black ass up off that seat."

When again there was no reply, Grout, using his pistol as a club, brought it down toward the man's head.

Here again eyewitness accounts differ. Some say the Negro raised his briefcase and the gun hit it, going off. Others say the Negro did not move at all and that the gun went off as the Sheriff was bringing it down to club him.

What is known is that the bullet ricocheted off something and struck Grout in the left shoulder.

Grout staggered out of the bus, bleeding profusely and shouting that he'd been shot. A crowd gathered quickly.

It became a mob. Somebody shouted, "That nigger shot the Sheriff!"

The mob of whites surrounded the bus. The white passengers got off. The Negro passengers, frightened, huddled in the rear, with the exception of the one Negro man who remained in his seat. He seemed utterly calm and some said he smiled slightly.

The mob started to throw rocks at the bus. Soon all the safety plate windows were spider-webbed and it became difficult to see inside.

Then someone shouted, "Let's get him!" And there was a surge toward the door of the bus.

But no one went in. Some said no one was able to get in—that some sort of invisible shield hurled back anyone who mounted past the first step.

The frustrated, howling mob, seemingly in a lynching mood, raged around the bus for half an hour until they were dispersed by the, arrival of the state police.

Cagle, the driver, was located and, with the state police escorting him, he drove the bus to Biloxi.

There the Negro man was questioned and finally released. He gave his name as Brown. He went to the home of the Rev. James Evander, a prominent Negro clergyman, to spend the night.

Cagle was reprimanded by the bus company, which said the Negro man had been entirely within his rights. A company spokesman said he did not know at the moment what it planned to do about the damage to its bus.

Sheriff Grout was reported to be in fair condition in the hospital.

I made only minor changes in the story before I sent it on to London, under a byline. I don't know what color Mr. Patterson, our Mount Pelley stringer, is. It isn't one of the questions we ask at World Wide. I suppose he'd have to be white in a place like that. But I'm sure Mr. Brown would have been glad to know he existed, to help balance Sheriff Grout.

All the people like us are We,
And everyone else is They.
—Rudyard Kipling

CHAPTER NINE
(JULY 30, WED.)

HIGH TOR, N.Y., is a pretty enlightened place. It's the hometown of artists, writers and theater people, budding and blooming. It has a syndicated political cartoonist whose satire is just a shade less biting than Herblock's. It has a playwright who has won a Pulitzer prize. It has a socially conscious novelist whose books are best sellers in spite of their Messages. Then there's the Chinese-American artist who not only prospers but (or perhaps I should say "and therefore") is a respected and socially accepted member of the community.

High Tor is progressive, forward-looking. It's quaint and countrified—though it's only 35 minutes from Times Square— because of its strict zoning laws. It has been written up in *The Exurbanites* as a place neither as intellectual nor as stuffy as Fairfield County, Connecticut, possibly because it doesn't have as many advertising men. It's not as rich, either, which is why Mae and I can afford to live there on the minimum plot allowed—one acre.

As I say, High Tor is no slouch of a town. If you're a New Yorker, but can't stand the city for the hundred-odd reasons I'm sure I don't have to list, High Tor is the place for you.

Therefore Mae and I were pretty shocked when we went out pub-crawling and did some unintentional eavesdropping.

I'd come home worn out from the eight-hour grind at WW, which had seemed like twelve, and suggested to Mae that we eat out and relax. She had the lamb chops back in the freezer and her second-best dress on in the same time it took me to luxuriate in an armchair over one dry martini.

All unwound, I put Mae in the Volkswagen and headed for Armando's, one of those quaint, but not too quaint, restaurants where the owner himself comes over and suggests. He suggested the veal cacciatore and we were agreeable.

As we were chewing the last mouthful, Armando came over to ask how it was.

"Great," I told him.

"Out of this world," Mae said.

"Delighted," Armando said. "But please don't mention those out-of-this-worlders to me."

"You mean the Monolithians?" I said. "What could they have possibly done to you?"

"Two of them came in for lunch today, disguised as Negro people."

"Oh?" Mae said.

"They weren't disguised," I told Armando. "There are Negroes on Monolithia, just as there are here."

"Well, anyway, I put them near the kitchen door and tell the girls to bump the chairs every time they come out. You know."

I hadn't known. I looked at Mae, who looked down at the remains of her veal cacciatore.

Armando went on: "So after a few bumps the one nearest the door makes with a finger to me. I ignore him, of course. Then he hollers, 'Armando!' The place is full of the luncheon trade. I frown, but what can I do? I hurry over to keep him quiet.

"'You are unhappy here?' I say to him. 'You would prefer to leave?' But he says 'No, we prefer a better table.' I tell him there are no other tables—the empty ones he sees are reserved. He says—he tells me this to my face—that this is a lie. I ask him to leave, so as not to create a disturbance.'"

"Sam," Mae said.

"Shh," I said. "Go on, Armando."

"Then he asks for the telephone, as if this is the Stork Club and I can plug it in at the table. I tell him the pay phone is near the cashier's desk, he can use it on his way out. Subtle, you see?"

"Then what?" I asked.

"He goes to the phone and calls SCAD in Albany!" SCAD is the state commission against discrimination. "He tells them the whole story at the top of his voice. It is mortifying. And now I am likely to lose my license and have to close up'—Or else cater to the colored trade. Mr. Kent, you are with a powerful news service. You know about these things. Tell me—what can I do?"

"You can give us our check, Armando," I said.

Armando became upset. "You are late. I am sorry. I should not tell you my troubles and take up your time. No—there is no check. You have been my guests. My pleasure."

"But not mine, Armando." I said. I dropped a ten-dollar bill on the table. "If you don't want it, leave it for the waitress. Good-by, Armando. Come on, Mae."

In the car Mae said, "Ten dollars was too much. I saw the menu. Seven-fifty, maybe."

"All right," I said. "Consider it a two-fifty contribution to the NAACP. We'll make it up by not eating there again."

"Okay," she settled back in the seat. The financial end of it settled, Mae said, "Good for you, Sam. The nerve of him, taking it for granted we thought the same way he does. Why it wasn't so long ago that he was a minority himself."

"The hell with him," I said. "Let's go get a drink."

Reno's Roost has a bar and a band and serves fried chicken or shrimp in a basket. It's run by an old army buddy of mine, Paul Reno. He gambled on the county opening up when they began building the Tappan Zee Bridge across the Hudson and his gamble paid off. The place was jumping.

We went in and looked around for a place to sit. The bar was filled. So were the booths and tables.

Paul came over from nowhere and said, "Sam! Where the hell you been? Hello, Mae. How's the gestation?"

"He's fine," Mae said. "Big crowd tonight."

"The biggest, now you're here. Here you are. Reserved for the Kents."

"This looks like your table, Paul," I said. "We don't want to send you back to work."

"Sit down," he said. "I'll come sit with you when my feet get tired. What'll you have? First round's on the house."

"I'll have a very weak Tom Collins, Paul," Mae said, "and I mean weak."

"Right you are, Mrs. K. Sam?"

"Scotch and soda, thanks."

"Strong, to even it out. Okay. Max!" He called a waiter and gave the order. He had Seven-Up himself. Paul never drinks on the job till 1 A.M.

"I see Oliver's still with you," I said. Oliver is one of the bartenders. He's a Negro. "We should have come here for dinner, Mae."

"Oliver's my right-hand man." Paul said. "Where did you eat, chumps?"

"Armando's," Mae said. "But I'd just as soon not talk about it."

"Armando's!" Paul said. "That ptomaine domain! What's the matter—you don't like chicken? If you don't like chicken we got shrimp. For you we even got tablecloths, if you insist. Armando's! Has he got a band?"

"He's got nothing," Mae said. "Who's playing tonight, Paul?"

"Tonight as always we have the Trans-Hudson Five, the finest aggregation west of Ossining, augmented by that rising young cornet star, Pete Kato."

"Japanese?" I asked.

"The rising son himself."

"Never heard of him."

"Just off the plane. He's here for kicks. I don't pay him, but maybe I will. He's not bad."

"Jazzman?" I asked.

"I don't know," Paul said. "Sometimes he sounds like Harry James. Sometimes he's Max Kaminsky. He's obviously listened to a lot of records. He's pretty derivative."

That's one of the things I appreciate about Paul Reno. Most of the time he sounds like Mr. Night Club himself, but then he comes out with a word like "derivative."

Paul went off to see how things were in the kitchen. As I mentioned, the place was crowded, with little space between tables. The band was between sets and I could overhear the people at the table behind me.

"…deliberately soften us up with all that mumbo-jumbo in the UN," a man's voice was saying. "Then they smuggle in a boat-load of colored behind our backs, as if we didn't have enough of our own already."

"And Chinks," another man's voice said.

"And Chinks," the first man agreed. "And Japs, I'll bet that was their plan all along. They're dumping their unwanted surplus population on us. It's a sneaking subversive thing to do and I wonder when Old Fathead Allison will wake up to the fact that they're playing him for a sucker."

"You used to think Gov was pretty good," a woman's voice said. "You voted for him."

"Never again. The country's going to the dogs. It has been for years, ever since Roosevelt. My God, Earl, do you know a Spic family is trying to move in down the road from us? Bunch of jabbering foreigners—must be a dozen of them. Can't even speak English."

"Now, Harvey," the same woman's voice said. "How can you talk that way? You've always been very pleasant to our maid and you like Oliver over there behind the bar."

"Exactly," he said. "'Over there behind the bar.' In his place."

This might very well be Oliver's place one day, I thought to myself. Paul Reno was hoping to open another place, given the right breaks, and he'd spoken to me about the possibility of putting Oliver in charge of this one.

Feeling one up on the people behind me, I quit eavesdropping and gave Mae a big smile.

"Well," she said. "Welcome back. What pleases you so all of a sudden?"

"Nothing," I said. "Just the happy thought that that bunch of WASPS behind me are going to be stung themselves sooner or later."

"Wasps?"

"Capital letters. White Anglo-Saxon Protestants. It's a term applied in certain quarters to a certain type."

"You're a White Anglo-Saxon Protestant," Mae said.

Paul Reno came back. "You will shortly be entertained by the greatest little combo this side of Suffern," he said. "I'll join you for the concert, if you're not engaged in pitching woo."

Mae laughed. "Sit down, Paul. The woo was pitched a long time ago. We've been discussing the state of the world."

"On your night out? Sam, can't you ever forget that deadline stuff?"

"I'm willing to now, if your Augmented Five ever get their horns out."

There were piano, drums, guitar, trombone and clarinet, plus Kato's cornet. The guitar man usually played trumpet. They did a good loud job, but I noticed that Kato appeared really comfortable only when he was taking a solo, such as the Berigan chorus of *I Can't Get Started* or the James version of *You Made Me Love You,* where he was not only derivative but imitative. In ensemble work he was terrible.

We decided we'd better go home after the band closed with *The Saints.* I had my 6 A.M. alarm clock in mind.

You came to me from out of nowhere
so why don't you go back where you came from?
—Abe Burrows song title

CHAPTER TEN
(JULY 21, THURS.)

I MANAGED to shut off the alarm and get up without disturbing Mae. I was having breakfast when the back door slammed open. We don't lock our doors in countrified, law-abiding High Tor.

"Uncle Sam, Uncle Sam!" It was six-year-old Harry Tyler, the son of our neighbors. "There's a spaceship in the woods!"

"What were you doing in the woods at this uncivilized hour?" I said, the neighborly avuncular instinct grabbing the wrong end of his remark. Then I said, "What? A spaceship? In the woods?"

"I went out to pick some strawberries for my breakfast," Harry said. "That's why I was in the woods. It's big and black and nobody saw me, I don't think."

"How do you know it's a spaceship?"

"Everybody knows what a spaceship looks like. It's big and black, just the way it's supposed to be. Come on and see it."

"Is your daddy up yet?" I asked Harry. Len Tyler usually gets up a few minutes after I do. "Did you tell him?"

"He's on vacation," Harry said. I'd forgotten. "He's still asleep. So's Mommy. Come on and see the spaceship, Uncle Sam."

I always feel very martial when Harry and the other kids in the neighborhood call me Uncle Sam. I feel that I have to uphold the honor of the Republic and Set an Example.

"Son," I said, "you're on. Let us go investigate this phenomenon."

A telescope hung in the back hall where it had been gathering dust since I gave up being a satellite watcher. It was a pretty good Japanese telescope, not expensive, but not cheap either. I took it down and wondered whether to look for my old souvenir machete for protection. But I decided that would be overdoing it.

We have about an acre of clear ground behind our house, then the woods begin. It's really an abandoned apple orchard, with the apple trees grown tall and neglected and other trees grown to a respectable height between them. A lot of sticker-bushes live there, too—tough, nasty: things with needle-sharp pines. I wished I'd brought the machete after all.

Harry and I had threaded our way a few hundred feet when I stopped. My left shirt sleeve was torn, my pants were wet up to the knees from the dew, and I was sweating.

"That's far enough, Harry," I said. "There's no spaceship here."

He was a few yards ahead, ducking under a spiny branch I'd have to lift out of the way at my peril.

"It's right over there, Uncle Sam," he said. "I think I see it now."

"Yeah? I'll go as far as you are, and if it's not there, young Marco Polo, we're turning back."

"Shh," he said. "Come on."

I joined him and looked. "Where?"

"Right there. Near that red apple there." He pointed.

There were thousands of red apples, fit only for making pies if the peeler had the patience to cut away the bad spots.

I followed his point and he was right. Nestled in among the trees was a big bulk of a thing, brownish gray. It certainly wasn't anything that had been in the woods before.

"Do you see any people?" I asked Harry.

"No. Let's go knock on their door."

"No!" I said. "Let's circle around and see what it looks like from the other side."

We circled. I managed to tear my other shirt sleeve on a sticker that also drew blood. Then for a while we made better progress along the bed of a sunken, abandoned road. We had kept the spaceship on our left and now I could see a huge clearing on the far side of it, strung over with some kind of camouflage netting.

"There they are!" Harry said.

"Quiet!" I said, pulling him down behind the lip of the old road. I was past caring about clothes now.

There were at least a dozen of them in the clearing. More were coming out of the open hatch of the spaceship. Apparently they hadn't heard us. I uncapped the telescope and looked.

They were wearing their native woolen cloaks and were setting up furniture in the clearing, which had been divided into room-size rectangles outlined on the bare ground with paint or strips of white cloth.

In addition to the chairs, tables, desks and bookcases they had a number of pieces of equipment, which vaguely resembled movie or television cameras.

"What are they doing, Uncle Sam?" Harry asked. "Let me look through the telescope."

"I don't know. It looks as if they're building movie sets. Maybe the walls will come later." I handed him the telescope.

"Look, they're coming out different now," Harry said, and I grabbed the telescope back.

Those stepping out of the hatch now were wearing Earthstyle clothes, and not carrying anything. But not all of the clothes looked American. There were men in wide-lapeled European suits, men in the white linen suits of tropical countries, men in the jodhpurs or dhotis of the Asian Indian, men in glittering military uniforms and men in drab, unadorned military jackets worn by the leaders of some totalitarian countries. They went to the various room-sized rectangles and sat or stood. No one was talking.

Then I looked closely at their faces. I almost dropped the telescope.

I saw the Prime Ministers of England and India, the leader of the United Arab Republic, the President of France and half a dozen other premiers or presidents, ex-, present or potential.

Gouverneur Allison was there for the United States, as was Rupert Marriner, the Secretary of State, and several other high administrative officials.

I was watching the Soviet Union's top men come out when I heard a noise behind us.

"Run!" I told Harry, getting up myself. "Run home and tell your daddy."

He hesitated. "Aren't you coming, Uncle Sam?"

"I'll go another way, to confuse them. Go on, now!"

Harry ran back along the sunken road. I started in the other direction. I hadn't taken twenty steps when a Monolithian in a woolen cloak rose up in front of me. I darted off sideways and ran into another one. There were five in all.

Escape would have been impossible even with the machete. Without speaking they escorted me toward the clearing.

Be good and you will be lonesome.
—Mark Twain

CHAPTER ELEVEN
(AUG. 1, FRI.)

I WOKE UP. It was completely dark. For a few seconds I stared up into the blackness, then turned on my side and tried to go back to sleep. But in a moment I realized I wasn't in my own bed and remembered that I was a prisoner.

Fully awake, I sat up. The room, becoming light in a gradual effulgence, revealed itself as a cube about nine feet on each side, furnished with two things—a seven-foot couch, covered with a coarse wool material, and me. There was nothing else. I couldn't trace the source of the light. I lay down and the light faded; I sat up and it came on again.

My wristwatch was gone and I had no idea how long it had been since my capture. I had been marched in silence to the clearing, passing through four or five of the wall-less rooms. No one had spoken as I was led to one of the hatches of the spaceship.

I had made various remarks as I was being taken in—such as "What's going on?" "You can't do this to me," "I've got to get to work, for pete's sake," and "Listen, will you?"—but my captors weren't conversation-minded.

I was led up a ramp and into the relatively dim interior of the spaceship. I had a recollection of narrow corridors and an occasional notice painted on the wall in some alien script. Then I was pushed into a cabin and the door closed behind me. My captors stayed outside, but there was a man in the room, sitting behind a long table in one of the two big chairs. He was wearing a woolen cloak. He was older than any of the bright young men I'd seen before, white haired and grave in expression. He was tossing a ball from hand to hand. It wasn't a baseball, but I had said, for no reason that I could remember now, "I'm a Braves fan myself."

He smiled and said, "Sit down," indicating the other chair. "Yankees."

"That's no team," I said, sitting down, "that's a machine."

"Be that as it may," he said, "you must wonder why we are here."

"Not at all," I said. "You're not on my property." I was saying whatever came into my mind. I think my idea was to discomfit him and provoke him into saying something he didn't plan to—something revealing.

He kept tossing the ball from hand to hand. It was about the size of a handball, hard and black but apparently not rubber.

He revealed nothing. "The dew is heavy in the morning," he said, looking at my soaked clothing. "And you've got a nasty scratch. Would you like something for it?"

"What have you got?" I asked. "Mendicants?" I was freely associating, having nothing better in mind.

"Oh, yes. Medicants *and* mendicants. Menders and vendors and buttons and bows. Pills and potions and ankle-length hose."

I decided this was part of an attempt to hypnotize me and looked away from his tossing ball.

"And Mendes-France," I said, "and Hugh Gaitskell and Krishna Menon."

"Not to mention Sam Kent," he said. "Here, catch."

He tossed the ball to me and in reflex I caught it.

I woke up in the nine-foot cube.

Somewhere between then and now I'd been stripped of my sopping clothes and garbed in one of their woolen cloaks. It didn't itch as I'd imagined it would. In fact, I was quite comfortable. I wasn't hungry or thirsty either. I judged by this that it had been only a few hours since I'd caught the ball, which apparently was some kind of knockout drop, and been transferred to this cubic prison and its automatic lighting.

I got off the couch and explored. The walls, floor and ceiling were made of a gray metallic substance, neither cold nor warm to the touch. The couch was nothing more than an extension of the floor—two feet high and seven feet long—with half a dozen thick brown woolen blankets over it. There was no crack or seam in any wall to indicate a door and no vent to bring in the clean air I was breathing. I sat down, baffled.

After a while I said, "Hey!"

There was no answer.

I lay down and the light went out. I sat up again. The light came on.

My cloak had no pockets. I took it off and, naked, turned it inside out. It taught me nothing. I put it back on and thought idly of smoking a cigarette. There are times when I sit at the news desk and words simply will not come unless I light a cigarette. It may be that I don't take a single puff after the first one, but the mere action of lighting the cigarette sets the old train of thought to operating. But now I couldn't have cared less if I never had a cigarette. Or a drink. Or food.

But my curiosity was still perking. I got to my feet and made another circuit of the little room. I found something I'd overlooked before. On one of the walls near a comer were two knobs, one above the other. They were set out a scant quarter inch from the wall and were of the same color and material.

"This opens the door," I told myself, turning the top one clockwise.

No door opened.

"Then this does," I said, turning the other one.

Instead I got music. I'd found a radio.

It was Perez Prado, that musical humorist, ripping out an unabashed Latinate romp through an old standard, giving it new excitement with his dramatic pauses and irreverent burps.

The Prado record ended and a recorded commercial came on:

"Ladies, stop tearing the end off the wrapper on a loaf of bread," was the message I got. From this exhortation to the ladies, I judged that this was daytime radio.

The next station was more informative: "Temperature now 75 degrees—bright and enjoyable. And we hope it's nice where you are this fine Friday morning…"

Friday! It had been Thursday when my neighbor's boy had led me through the apple orchard. I wondered if young Harry had reported my capture, and if he had, whether anybody believed him.

My next thought was of Mae. She must be worried sick about me. She wouldn't have worried till suppertime yesterday, when I didn't get home on time—unless the office had called her to find out why I hadn't come to work, as it probably had. That meant she'd already had 24 hours of anxiety. I banged on the walls with my palms, then kicked with the flat of my bare foot, but no one came.

"Can't stay in bed?" the radio asked me. "Get up and still get five stay-in-bed benefits."

I turned the volume up as high as it would go, hoping that would attract the attention of my captors. But the rest of the booming commercial and the ensuing rendition of *Stardust*—a song I can do without—did nothing but hurt my ears.

I reduced the volume for a panegyric to "the most delightfully different cigarette ever made" and reflected that in spite of the fact that my own pack was gone with my clothes I didn't want to smoke.

Nor was I thirsty, I realized during subsequent commercials praising the joys of Coke and Seven Up. And I wasn't hungry, not reacting to the one about there being "more crackling good taste in every slice"—meaning bacon. And fortunately, considering the john-less aspect of my cell, I didn't have to go to the bathroom. My appetites seemed to have vanished with the 24 hours that had gone out of my life since I caught that handball in the alien's office.

What were they doing to me? I wondered. What had they done to me? I paced the limited confines of my prison, occasionally banging on the hard wall, then threw myself on the couch. As I lay down the lights went out and the radio faded. I sat up. The lights came on again and the radio woke lip to say:

"Time for news from American—live at 55! The news in just a moment."

"From Hackensack, New Jersey, an interesting sidelight on the aliens," the voice was saying in the verbless way of radio newsmen. "Commuters, faced with a new fare increase totaling 81 per cent in ten months, revolted against the Susquehanna Railroad today and rode to work in a bus provided by the Monolithians. They pay $24 a month instead of the $35 the new railroad fare would have cost. There was no immediate comment from the Susquehanna, but a spokesman from the commuters' association said the idea is so successful that a second group is joining…"

That being the first news item, it was obvious that nothing startling had been going on. Whatever all those duplicate men were planning to do, they hadn't done it yet.

"In Boston, a group of alien volunteers pitched in with a will to help tow away illegally parked cars. In the first two hours they towed away 28 unmarked police cars…"

WABC's newscast came five minutes before the hour. I switched to the NBC station, "where news comes first"— meaning on the hour—and endured the opening gongs, which were NBC's substitute for big black headlines. It started off with a couple of non-Monolithian items from overseas.

"More news in a moment. But first—

"Isn't there someone, somewhere, whose voice you'd like to hear? Well then, why not pick up your telephone…"

I yelled at it, "Yes, God damn it! Why don't I just?" and switched it off.

I must have fallen asleep. I came to in darkness and when I sat up the lights glowed on. I tried the radio again. Music.

I still wasn't hungry or thirsty and I still didn't have to go to the bathroom. I wondered if I were being watched. I looked again for a possible tiny television eye but couldn't see any. I considered thumbing my nose in all directions, as a morale factor, but decided it would be undignified.

I wondered what time it was, how long I'd slept. Somehow it sounded like early evening music, suitable for housewives preparing dinner and men driving home from a hard day at the office.

Then station identification told me it was seven o'clock (P.M.) and asked whether right about here I would like a beer. The answer was no. All I wanted was to get out.

"And now we bring you that popular round-table discussion of events of the day, *News and Newsmen,*" the radio said, "featuring the men who edit the news for leading papers and wire services. Tonight our subject is 'Monolithians—Friend or Foe?' and our panel consists of Russell Sidenam, city editor of the *World-Telegram;* Barton Pascal, reporter on the *Daily News;* Herb Small, from the world desk of the Associated Press; and Sam Kent, assistant editor of the New York bureau of World Wide News…"

A few minutes later, after the inevitable commercial, I heard my own voice passionately defending the Monolithians as men of principle and high conscience whose only purpose was to uplift their brethren on Earth to a realization of their manifest destiny as worthy members of the community of the Interstellar Realm.

> Some circumstantial evidence is very strong,
> as when you find a trout in the milk.
>
> —Thoreau

CHAPTER TWELVE
(AUG. 2, SAT.)

I HAD PUT MYSELF to sleep by playing the name game. You start with two A's, as in Alfred Adler, then go to AB, Anthony Boucher, and so on—Arthur Clarke, Antal Dorati, Albert Einstein, Alexander Fleming. I dropped off somewhere in the middle of the C's—Mickey Cohen or Norman Corwin—and woke up knowing exactly where I was and wondering what time it was.

It turned out to be 8 A.M., August 2d, according to Station WTRU, which was playing wake-up music for the poor souls who had to work on Saturday, and a fine warm day it looked like it would be. For me it looked like it would be the same kind of cooped-in day, with nothing to do but chomp at the bit and wax wroth at the aloof jailers who had stolen my identity and sent it out to make me look ridiculous. He who steals my purse steals trash, I thought, but he who steals my good name... They'd stolen both, these alien do-gooders with their sweet mad reasonableness.

"They said it couldn't be done—couldn't be done!" the radio boomed.

Well, they done did it. I didn't know how, but they duplicated me and sent me out to champion their cause while the original model languished helpless in their cell, beset by commercials—and growing a fine beard.

"Our traffic-conditions helicopter reports unusual tie-ups in various suburban areas," WTRU was saying. "Traffic is bumper-to-bumper and backed up for miles in some sections... For a direct report we go to our beeper-phone and we'll see if we can talk to the police department in Haverstraw, New York, close to the scene of one of the major tie-ups on Route 9W."

I perked up at that. Haverstraw is near High Tor on the west bank of the Hudson River.

"My engineer tells me we've got Sergeant Kiefer of the Haverstraw police on the beeper-phone. Go ahead, Sergeant Kiefer! Tell us, what's the cause of the big traffic jam on Route 9W?"

Sergeant Kiefer came in, loud, clear and profane. "Some God damn jerks are obeying the 20-mile speed limit," he said.

"Heh, heh, Sergeant Kiefer," the announcer said. "Remember, you're on the beeper-phone. This is radio, you know! What's that you say about the speed limit?"

"The speed limit's 20 miles an hour and there's two cars abreast on the highway not going any faster. Traffic's backed up clear to Piermont to the south."

"Piermont to the south," the announcer repeated, just as if it meant something to him. "How about in the other direction, Sergeant?"

"Same God damn thing. Two other wise guys ambling along—"

"You're on the air, Sergeant!"

"Same thing, I mean. They're backed up north to Bear Mountain. It's murder."

"Why don't you arrest them, Sergeant?"

"For what? For obeying the speed limit? It'd make more sense to arrest the stupid jerks that posted the 20-mile limit on a state highway."

"Just a minute, Sergeant! We're getting a message from our WTRU traffic-conditions helicopter that the lead cars, both northbound and southbound, have banners reading 'Monolithians Obey the Law.' Can you confirm that, Sergeant? Is it true that the Monolithian space people are the instigators of this fantastic traffic tie-up up there in—in—what county is that up there where you are anyway, Sergeant?"

"Rockland County. Yeah. That's what their signs says. One of the cars is a Volkswagen and there's some guy in it says he's a reporter. Sam Kent of World Wide. Legal Sam, the law-abiding man, he told us he was. You know him?"

"I've heard of World Wide, Sergeant. It's one of the three wire services we have here at WTRU to give you and all our listeners the most complete, up-to-the-minute news of any station in the metropolitan area. You say a reporter is personally instigating this mass traffic tie-up?"

"He's legal. We can't touch him. You want to know anything else? I got to get back to work here."

The announcer let him go back to work because he had to go back to work himself—to wit, to put on a commercial about something that was more lastingly odor-free than any other something.

So my alter ego had stolen not only my good name but my little red Volkswagen as well. I hoped he was keeping it in second for his 20-mile-an-hour jaunt and not ruining the gearbox by trying to do 20 in third.

Then a more urgent thought occurred to me. Had Spurious Sam, the Duplicated Man, gone home last night and posed as the lawful wedded husband of Mae Kent? If that was the case I wasn't even missing, and no one would ever have investigated young Harry's story of my capture.

"Let me out of this God damned trap!" I yelled, getting as profane as Sergeant Kiefer. Nobody paid any attention.

My attention wandered during the next news item, which was about a cabinet crisis in one of the Arab states, and I began to think about my stomach. I still wasn't hungry, but a peculiar sensation was setting in. I can only describe it as a hunger to be hungry.

I was also experiencing a thirst to be thirsty. For a while I kept saying to myself, "You get more beer in your beer in New Jersey"—parroting the words of one of the few clever commercials I had heard. I stopped doing that when it began to sound idiotic—but then I started asking myself: "Right about here wouldn't you like a beer?" and the answer was almost beginning to be yes.

This led to my becoming cigarette-conscious. My mind flitted from one slogan to another. Twenty thousand filter traps (or was it 40,000?). You can light either end. Protects the T-Zone. Independent laboratory tests prove… Reach for a Lucky instead of a sweet. (I wasn't even old enough to smoke when that one was current.) I'd walk a mile for a Camel. Travels the smoke further. Wherever particular people congregate…

Stop it, I told myself. You don't want a cigarette (wanting one). You don't want a drink, Sam; they teetotalled you (but it was wearing off). Why not go out to dinner tonight? (Medium rare, waiter; and lots of mushrooms.) And then Mae—Mae, Mae! I wanted my cute little pregnant wife, walking around flat-footed in her maternity blouse and smiling secretly to herself over our burgeoning child.

It was right about here that the radio man dug out and started to play an extremely associative song of Mae's and mine—*Who's Your Little Whoozis*. And then I blacked out.

I have been in such a pickle
since I saw you last.
—Shakespeare

CHAPTER THIRTEEN
(AUG. 3, SUN.)

I WASN'T in my cell any more. I was lying back in an armchair in a large comfortable-looking room. There was one other person in it, a kindly looking middle-aged man in another armchair next to a wall under a painting of a country scene, with trees and cows and a sky studded with tiny clouds.

"Hello," the man said. "I am Mox." He was wearing one of those Monolithian cloaks. "How are you?"

I felt too weak to answer. I tapped my finger on the arms of the chair and the effort made me terribly tired. I closed my eyes again.

"Lunch is about to be served," Mox said. "Perhaps you would care to freshen up first? To shave?"

I opened my eyes and rubbed a hand over my cheeks. They were pretty whiskery.

"How are you fixed for blades?" I said. Don't ask me why. One gets conditioned.

"Amply," Mox said. He made a gesture with his left hand and somebody in another woolen cloak came in with shaving equipment, put it on a table at my elbow and went out, bowing.

I looked at the steaming bowl of hot water, the tube of shaving cream (brush versus jar, I thought, remembering the old ad), the razor and mirror. I looked in the mirror, expecting the worst. The beard was pretty heavy and the cheeks under it looked more sunken than I'd remembered. But my eyes were clear and my tongue looked normal.

"There will be no deleterious effects," Mox said. "You'll be good as new after your lunch."

"Lunch? What time is it?"

He seemed to do a mental conversion before he replied: "Twelve-seventeen P.M. Eastern Daylight Saving Time; 1617 Greenwich."

"And an hour later on the Rue de la Paix," I said. "I'll have the snails and some Beaujolais." I was feeling lightheaded.

"Interesting," he said, watching me with an encouraging smile.

"But irrelevant. I couldn't eat snails on an empty stomach. I just said that because it rhymes. What have you got for American times?"

"Lamb chops," Mox said, looking at me closely now, "baked potato, broccoli, tossed salad, strawberry shortcake and coffee. Or—"

"That's for me. Stop right there. Can I have it now and shave later? I'm starved."

"Certainly. Without further ado." Mox raised his right hand again and the same man came in, though he couldn't have seen the signal, wheeling a tray. An almost overpoweringly delicious smell reached my nostrils and I shivered a little in my chair.

Mox got up. "I'll leave you while you fall in," he said. I didn't answer him, being busy taking the covers off the serving dishes. I suppose he meant "fall to," which I did, with a will.

My curiosity returned as I appeased my appetite. Having wolfed down the meat and vegetables with hardly a conscious thought, I went through the salad in more leisurely fashion, rehearsing questions to ask Mox. I positively dawdled over the cake and coffee, it having just occurred to me that this could be the equivalent of the doomed man's last meal.

"Look, Mox," I said when he came back. "Thanks all the same, but I don't think I'll shave. Just give me my clothes and I'll go now. No; don't bother. I'll go as I am. I don't live very far. Oh—and thanks for the lunch."

Mox smiled and sat down. "You're a very amusing man, Mr. Kent. We couldn't possibly let you go. We have great plans for you."

"Plans?" The well being induced by the lunch began to seep away. "Like what?"

"Details later. First we should discuss the terms of your employment. The salary will be substantial, so there'll be no problem there, but you might be interested in the fringe benefits, such as the size of your paid-up life insurance policy, the beneficiaries…"

"Now, look. I haven't said I'd join your organization…"

"Ah, but you've already joined. We had planned to come to you, but you saved us that trouble. You came to us voluntarily and have already taken part in one of our minor Missions—that of working for the repeal of antiquated traffic laws."

"I did not. That wasn't me."

"Who would believe you? You previously espoused our cause on a nationwide radio-and-television program."

"That wasn't me either, and you know it. I don't know how you did it, but that double you rigged up isn't going to be able to get away with it much longer."

"I think he can. You see, Sam, for all practical purposes that double, as you call him, *is* you. There's nothing about you that he doesn't know and everything he does or says is perfectly in character with what you would do or say—presupposing one slight shift in motivation. And you may be sure that adjustment has been made."

"You mean you've been picking my brains all the time you had me cooped up in that cell?"

"You could put it that way. Not all the time, of course. Only while you slept. We know as much about you as you do about yourself. More, probably, because we've probed your subconscious as well as your surface self-awareness."

"Oh yeah? What was my mother's maiden name?"

"Clemens," Mox said instantly. "Hence your full name, with its literary if not strictly genealogical connection—Samuel Langhorne Clemens Kent. You know you are not directly related to Mark Twain, of course?"

"I was told I was," I said defensively. "Way back."

"Way, *way* back, perhaps," Mox said. "Not in any modern sense."

"That's no proof that you read my mind. There must be genealogical tables…"

"Certainly. But there are no written records of the time you stole money from the newsstand outside the candy store in Ozone Park."

"I never…" I started to say before I remembered. I'd been about ten. The way to do it was to scoop up the coins boldly on your way into the store and hand them to the owner while buying a candy bar or a roll of caps. Of course you palmed a dime or so on the way. I'd never told anybody about it and I felt suffocated in shame.

"Or the seventy-five wingless flies in the mayonnaise jar," Mox said relentlessly. "You were trying for a hundred, weren't you? But you got sick to your stomach. Or the time you sold your brother's bicycle and claimed it had been stolen. Or the college exams with the dates written in your palm. Or…"

"Stop it! That's enough!"

"I don't condemn you, Sam. No one is wholly free of blame. I have not mentioned these things to bring you pain but to prove to you that the Monolithian Sam Kent is as aware of your potentialities as you are yourself. He has done nothing you would not do, given the proper conviction or opportunity."

I couldn't look at him. "Swiping a dime off a newsstand isn't the same thing as betraying your country," I said miserably.

"It would depend, wouldn't it, on which was the greater good? If the dime you stole bought a quart of milk for your family during the depression when your father was out of work—if the candy store man was obviously better off—if your country were Nazi Germany—"

"The United States isn't Nazi Germany," I said. I could reject that one, at least.

"True," Mox said. "But I said 'if.' You're a man of perception. You don't need an overt act, such as six million deaths, to persuade you that something is wrong. You see it every day in the news reports that are your business—in the United Nations debates on nuclear testing, in the reports on the strontium-90 in food, in the disfigured Hiroshima women getting plastic surgery, in the perennial radiation scares."

"Is that what you're up to?" I asked him. "You think we're going to wipe ourselves out and you're altruistically going to preserve us? You're going to step in and run our world for us because you think we're not capable of handling our own affairs?"

"If necessary," he said.

"The end justifies the means, you think. You have no faith in our ability not to commit suicide."

"Not as much as you seem to have. Look, Sam, we've got a job for you to do and we'd like you to take it because you want to. It would be better for all of us that way. But if you are reconsidering your decision to volunteer, we have ways of conscripting you."

"Torture?" I tried to speak calmly. "Brainwashing?"

"Neither you nor anyone else will ever be tortured. As for the other, we'd prefer that you washed your own brain of its misconceptions about us. Try to realize that what we are trying to do—and what we will do—is for your own good and for the good of all of us."

He was the soul of sincerity, this Mox. I was relieved about the torture. I was even half tempted to believe the other things. But I wasn't going to brainwash myself or anybody else.

On the other hand, I could let him think I'd been won over and bore from within whenever I got the chance. The standard injunctions to the prisoner of war were no longer name-rank-and-serial-number. That had gone out after the lessons of the Korean war. The new instructions were to lie. Tell them whatever they wanted to hear. Confess to anything, no matter how outrageous. Embrace the enemy with lies until he had no idea where the truth lay. I decided to try it, but not so fast as to arouse suspicion.

"If I do volunteer," I said, after a period of what I hoped appeared to be profound thought, "will I be able to see my wife?"

"Of course," Mox said, beaming at me.

"I'm more worried about her than I am about strontium-90," I said ingenuously. "She's going to have a baby."

"How marvelous."

"Her name is Mae," I said. "We haven't been married long and this will be our first child."

"Congratulations."

"A man's got to think of his family first," I said, pouring it on, "doesn't he?"

"Absolutely."

"I mean it's all very well to expect every man to do his duty, but where does that duty lie? We've signed a treaty of peace and friendship with you, haven't we? Through the UN, I mean. And if that's good enough for the President, I guess it's good enough for me. Poor Mae. She must be worried to death. I've got to see her."

"And so you shall, Sam."

"That's all I ask. I volunteer. We've got to stop this ridiculous experimentation with the very seeds of our own destruction." I was washing the old brain with everything I had. "What's the job you have for me?"

I hoped I hadn't overdone it. But Mox was beaming.

"I am happy to inform you," he said, "that the position is that of press secretary to President Gouverneur Allison."

"My, you're home early," Mae said, giving me a kiss.

It wasn't a big, fat oh-I'm-so-glad-to-see-you're-safe kiss. Not at all. I looked at my watch: it was a little after 3 P.M. Early? Here it was Sunday. Mae hadn't seen me since Thursday night and she said I was home early. Had the Monolithians played a trick with time? Was it only Friday afternoon?

"Listen, Mae," I said. "Did you watch your story today? What happened after this girl with the amnesia walked into Dr.

Kindfellow's office, not realizing he was the very one she had fled a thousand miles to avoid?" Mae watches this television serial come hell or high water. It's one of her few vices.

"Silly," Mae said. "You know it's not on on Sunday. I thought you wouldn't be home till six. We were just going to take our nap."

"You thought I wasn't going to be home till six? Is that what I told you?" I was feeling my way, full of inklings and forebodings.

"Well, you usually get home at six when you're on the day shift—or is it five-thirty on weekends when you drive right in? Anyway, you're early. I'm glad. I guess we can skip our nap. Do you want to eat early?"

All I wanted to do was get to the bottom of this. It was beginning to be obvious that this double of me that the Monolithians whipped up actually had been living in my house as well as doing my job. I wanted to ask a dozen questions—but I couldn't without either giving Mae a terrific shock or making her think I was out of my mind.

"No, I'll eat whenever it's ready. Listen, Mae—have I been acting strange lately? I mean in the last couple days?"

"I've got some nice lamb chops for supper. Strange? Well, no stranger than usual, Sam. I mean, you've been a little bit nutty ever since the spacemen came. Naturally I've made allowances. I guess it's a pretty big story and a person has to take sides the way you did on that TV show."

"Oh, you saw that, did you?"

"Well, of course I did! You said only last night how the check will pay for the play pen and the bathinette. Surely you remember that?"

"Sure I do," I lied. "It wasn't awfully much, I guess."

"Fifty dollars is what you said it was. It helps."

"Sure. What else did I say?"

"When?"

"Last night."

"You said—honestly, Sam, are you sure you're all right?—you said we'd take an early vacation next year and go to Bermuda, all three of us."

"Sure, Bermuda," I said. "Sure I'm all right. I'm sorry, Mae; I've been a little confused ever since I got my new job."

"What new job? You didn't tell me that."

"No, I guess I didn't. It wasn't set until today. I'm leaving World Wide. I'm going to be press secretary to the President."

Mae did a double take—or at least a double blink—and said without more than a second's hesitation: "Isn't that wonderful!"

"I guess so," I said.

"What do you mean you guess so? It's marvelous! Of course you did say once you didn't think much of Gov. I think you said he doesn't have a brain in his head. Isn't that the way you put it?"

"I may have made some such remark," I said. "Such a thought has crossed my mind. But now I'm in a position to help him. I may even be able to put a thought or two into his head. I'll be the chief factotum of the White House mimeograph machines—the disseminator, if not molder, of executive policy. Then there's the big old unsneezable fact that it pays a fast eighteen thousand a year."

Mae's eyes went sort of glazy and I could see her trying to divide that mentally by 52. "That's a lot, isn't it?" she said finally. "Now we can afford to replace that storm window that fell out last winter and maybe repaper the nursery."

"We can take care of the storm window, anyway. It's the least we can do for whoever rents the place when we move to Washington."

"Oh—of course. I forgot we'd have to move to Washington."

"I don't see any way out of it. It's a little too far for commuting."

> They are waiting on the shingle—will
> you come and join the dance?
> —The Mock Turtle

CHAPTER FOURTEEN
(AUG. 4, MON.)

My APPOINTMENT with Frij was for one P.M. Mox had telephoned on Sunday night and told me about it. He didn't say who Frij was. He merely gave me the address and the room number and hung up.

Frij had an office on the thirty-ninth floor of a building on Fifth Avenue in the forties. He had, in fact, the entire penthouse. A small plaque on the front door said simply: PEERLESS PROMOTIONS.

I rang the bell.

The door opened and a tall gray-haired man grabbed my hand.

"I'd know you anywhere, Sam. Come in, old man. Frij is the name. Frij by name but warm by nature. Like a drink?"

I suppose he was punning on the. British nickname for a refrigerator. "Not right now, thanks," I said.

Frij wore a dark, pin-stripe suit, a plaid waistcoat and bow tie. He looked about forty-five. He was solidly built, like a football player gone only slightly to pot. He nodded and half closed one eye.

"Very smart," he said. "I admire your restraint. Sit down, old man." He indicated a deep leather chair on the visitor's side of the huge wooden desk. He dropped himself into a swivel chair on his side, leaned back and propped his feet on a corner of the desk, which was clear of everything except two telephones and three animal figurines made of heavy-looking black plastic. I recognized two of them. One was an elephant and the other was a donkey. I couldn't figure out the third, which was bigger that either of the others. It must. have been some kind of Monolithian animal.

It seemed to be up to me to say something, so I said, "Nice place you have here. Quite a view." And so it was. The Empire State Building loomed up to the south and Rockefeller Center to the north. The third set of windows gave a good view of the Hudson River.

"Without a peer," Frij said. "Peerless, in a word. Peerless Promotions. That's us. My name, I've decided after considerable thought, will be Addison Madison. What do yon think of it, old man?"

I thought very little of it but I pretended to turn it over in my mind. "It's got class," I said finally. To myself I thought, *With a capital K.*

"Exactly," Addison Madison-Frij said. "That's what they want—class. Frij is too alien-sounding for their ears. They must have something that inspires confidence."

"Confidence in what, if I may ask?"

"Ask by all means. That's what I want you to do. Ask and criticize and suggest. This thing must roll, on all sixteen. It must purr, like the contented kitten. Or is it cow? I need you, old man, I tell you frankly. The closest kind of collaboration is necessary if we are to achieve our objective."

He took his feet off the desk and sat up purposefully in his chair. "If you follow me."

"Not entirely," I said. "What exactly are you promoting? Public acceptance of Monolithia?"

"Secondarily," he said, giving me a sincere, old-school-tie look. "President Allison primarily. Through him, us. Didn't Mox brief you?"

"Only briefly. I thought you were going to fill in the gaps."

"That I will," Frij said. "But in good time. First lunch. Then there's the cocktail party. Both excellent gap-fillers. There's no urgency at all." He rang and a girl came in. A pretty girl, about five-feet-four and black-haired, wearing horn-rimmed glasses and carrying a notebook.

"Joy," he said, "put down in your book that you're to take Mr. Kent to lunch and keep him occupied until it's time for the party. Joy, Sam. Sam, Joy Linx. That's all for now, Sam. See you at the party."

I followed Joy out, not unwillingly.

At her desk she took a manila envelope from a drawer and counted out two hundred dollars. "I'm an old-fashioned girl, Mr. Kent," she said. "You take *me* out to lunch." And she pushed the bills over to me.

"What's this?"

"Expense money. There's more when that runs out."

"Want me to sign for it?"

"No. That's petty cash; it's off the books already."

We took a cab to the Algonquin and sat next to each other on the leather couch along one wall and had Scotches and made small talk about the waiter with the two-foot-high pepper grinder and the old Thanatopsis and Inside-Straight Society that used to meet there.

Joy Linx spelled her last name for me, emphasizing that it had no "y," and took off her glasses. She said to call her Joy. You can say all you want about glasses not hiding a girl's beauty, but Joy was much more of a looker without them. "I'm near-sighted," she said, "and they're heavy."

"I approve," I said. "How long have you been with Peerless Promotions, Joy?"

"With the aliens, you mean? You can speak frankly. They hired me last Friday and I started today. How about you, Mr. Kent?"

I told her to call me Sam, but decided not to say, as I was tempted to, that I wasn't sure I was with the aliens, exactly, even though, I was on their payroll. "I started today, too, officially," I said. "It's been very pleasant work so far. Another Scotch?"

"Just one more," she said, and we smiled at each other a bit stiffly and tentatively.

I ordered the second round and the lunch, trying not to look at the prices. They were academic, of course, considering the expense money in my pocket, but I couldn't help contrasting this with my hectic lunches at World Wide—often a sandwich brought down from the cafeteria and eaten on the desk with a cup of office-brewed coffee—total cost under half a dollar.

I risked telling Joy about this. You never know what kind of reception such a sad little anecdote may have and I was relieved when she laughed with genuine understanding.

"I used to do the same thing," she said. "Only I brought my own sandwich. I liked egg salad on whole wheat."

"I'm a liverwurst and swiss cheese on rye man myself. With lettuce and mustard. Who were you with before Peerless?"

"A theatrical agency. I had some far-fetched dream of becoming an actress by association one day."

"You've certainly got the looks for it."

"Thanks, Sam, but I'm afraid my only talent lies in being a secretary."

I made some gallant reply, then asked what she did, exactly, for Frij—alias Addison Madison.

"Isn't that a scream of a name?" Joy said. "So far all he's told me is that I'm to be his Girl Friday—I guess he picked that up when he was studying his role. And to take you out to lunch. It's a fine job." Joy looked straight at her plate of *beef au jus* and said, "I suppose you're married."

"Yes," I said, looking at my scallops.

"Just like to get the facts. I'm divorced, myself. Incompatibility. Linx is his name. I kept it because it's more euphonious, professionally, than Kaplan."

"I see."

"I wish you much better luck, Sam."

"Thanks," I said, and almost told her Mae was pregnant. For some reason I didn't. I don't think it was entirely because I was reluctant to compare her unhappy state with my excellent one. Joy was a very pretty girl indeed. "Thanks," I said again, and left it at that. "How about another drink?"

"Okay." She looked up and smiled. "Forgive the personal history."

"Not at all." I got the waiter's eye and ordered, and a busboy took away the plates. "Tell me about this cocktail party. Who all's coming??"

"Some of everybody, I gather. Everybody who is anybody, that is."

"Oh? Big names?" I didn't know anything about the social life of the aliens, come to think of it. So far all I was familiar with was their public appearances, in a news sense, and their cloak-and-dagger intrigues, such as locking me up in that air-conditioned dungeon.

"The biggest," Joy said. "You'll see. They've been mingling like mad."

"What for, I wonder."

"Your guess is as good as mine. Ten times better, probably."

"Will you be going to the party??"

"Yes. In my Girl Friday capacity. Wearing my glasses, so I can recognize people across the room, and seeing that Addison Madison shakes hands with everybody."

"How about shaking hands with me now, just in case you're too busy later?"

"I won't be," Joy smiled. But she put her hand in mine. I neglected to give it back right away.

Then the drinks came and after a while Joy put her glasses on and we took a cab back to the office. She sat on her side and I sat on mine and we talked about the weather. It was hot.

The party had got to the point where everybody seemed to be talking at once. Enough liquor had been consumed for the initial tentativeness to have worn off and the Monolithians were no longer standing apart as they had been at the beginning. It was impossible to tell who was from where, except that the women were all from Earth, presumably, and I heard several variations on the question, "Are you one of Them or one of Us?"

The din of the talk, the overworked air conditioners and the mechanics of barkeeping made every conversation a private one within its own area, even though it was carried on at the top of the voice.

"I'm one of us," I shouted to a short, stout martini fellow who cornered me in an alcove where I'd gone to put out a cigarette. "Sam Kent, World Wide." I'd forgotten for the moment that I'd resigned.

"John Blobber," the martini said. "I'm with the Yarbutta people." That's what it sounded like. "Good name, Sam. Sam Clemens, Sam Goldwyn, Sam Spade. Lots of people named Sam. Sam Levene, Sam Behrman—good American name."

"I never thought it wasn't, Mr. Yarbutta," I told him, trying to edge away.

"No. John Blasher," he said, approximately. "I'm *with* the Yollawa people."

"Oh, sure. I guess I've heard about them."

"Make tunsleys," he said, waving his glass dangerously in my vicinity. "Business very good, at the moment, thanks to the Monolithians." He set his glass down on the little wooden table that held the ashtray I'd sought out, knocked on the wood and picked up his glass. "Sam F. B. Morse—great inventor. Sam Lincoln, great preshident."

"I think you've got that last one wrong," I said, backing off. "Fellow named Abe, he was, I believe. Look, Mr. Blasher, you just reminded me—I've got to see Abe Copeless about that story in Hammerslam this morning. You know the one I mean."

I left him nodding in polite confusion. At the bar I got a fresh Scotch and turned around to find myself trapped in a group playing Real Names.

"You with the Scotch," a red-haired woman said. "You can't go till you tell us who Archibald Leach is."

"Cary Grant," I said instantly out of my storehouse of copyreader's lore. I tried to go, but the woman put a hand on my drinking arm and said, "Oh, this is one we've got to keep. I'll bet you don't know Joe Yule, Junior."

"Why, madam," I said, "everyone knows Mickey Rooney."

"This man is a gem," the woman—she was a gin and tonic—said,

"Arlington Brugh?"

"S. Arlington Brugh," I corrected. "Robert Taylor. Now may I go?" I smiled, so she wouldn't think my rude question was rude.

"Not a chance, my dear boy. You're an absolute fount. Irwin, give him that one that stumped us before." Irwin was a tall, lean Screwdriver.

"Lucille LeSueur," he said defiantly, wrinkling an eyebrow.

"Joan Crawford," I told him instantly.

The gin-and-tonic lady shrieked with glee—"That's right I We all guessed Lucille Ball. How do you do it?"

"It's really very simple," I said modestly. "You see, I'm their lawyer and they have no secrets from me."

"I doubt that very much," the third Real Names player said frostily. He was a Bloody Mary and I figured it served him right. "James Stewart," he said, as if he were playing the ace of spades. "Let's see you get out of that."

"You're doing it backwards," the gin lady said reprovingly.

"No, I'm not," the Bloody Mary man insisted.

"No, he's not," I said, lifting my Scotch and her arm for a sip. "That's Stewart Granger. And Charles Pratt is Boris Karloff and Rita Hayworth is Margarita Cansino, and Roy Rogers is Leonard Slye and—if you will unhand me, my good woman—Frederick Bickel is Fredric March."

"Don't let him get away," she shrieked. "He's priceless!" But I did get away. I weaved my way among clusters of people who were making sounds of our time touching on Lorca, Kerouac, Glenn Gould, Lenny Bernstein, Brendan Behan, Sinatra, Astaire, Gielgud, Philip, Kennedy, Marlon, Ingrid, and Marilyn, and found myself cheek by jowl with my old friend Eurydice Playfair, who used to be a newspaper-woman herself.

My Real Names ploy, which I had been savoring along with my umpteenth Scotch, turned to ashes as it recalled itself forcibly to me that I was no better than dear Riddie, having sold out to the aliens myself.

"Dear boy!" she said. "Where have you been keeping yourself?"

"Between you and me, Riddie," I said, "between the devil and the deep blue tax collector, up to just about now. Can I get you a drink?"

This is one way of vanishing. You just don't come back from the bar. It's understandable at such a conclave. But Riddie was not to be put off that easily.

"I'm well fixed, Samuel, my old," she said, waving three-quarters of a bourbon on the rocks at me. "What I want to know is who's running the store, now that Kent and doubleyou doubleyou have phfft? Not old pinchpurse Hyatt, surely?"

"I have put all those mundane cares behind me," I said in an attempt to be sprightly. "Greater things are afoot."

"How very true," she said. Riddie was dressed to the hilt in a lame thing that clung to her well-preserved curves. "I'm delighted you've got yourself a handhold. There's room enough for all."

"Listen, Riddie," I said, "I know you can't tell the Mono-lithians without a scorecard, they're so assimilable, but what the good hell is the object of all this? For what greater gain is the tab being picked up? What's the deal, old pal? Spill; will you?"

"You're too suspicious, Sam. This is conviviality rampant. We drink and be merry and ask not the reason why. Live, man! Pluck the daisies while you may. How is Mae, by the way?"

"Just fine," I said. "Just absolutely fine. That's an interesting philosophy you have there, about plucking."

Riddie gave me a close look. "How many have you had, my friend? How about a sandwich?"

"Don't worry," I told her. "I'm not going to disgrace anybody. I've had three, is all." Besides miscounting I was ignoring the three I'd had at lunch with Joy Linx.

"Well, maybe," Riddie said. She acknowledged a high sign from somebody (an alien?) at the other side of the room and said quickly, "Don't worry about a thing. If you have any problems, just take them to Mox or Frij. Or me. I've got to run now, Sammy."

And she was off.

I made for the farther bar across the room, where I'd spotted Joy Linx.

Joy had changed from her severe lunchtime suit into a low-cut black satin, which matched her hair and did all kinds of things for her figure. I cannot tell a lie and say I hadn't noticed this figure heretofore, but hadn't had the opportunity to notice it to such advantage. Bee-lining, I reached her side.

"Your recent acquaintance presents his compliments," I said, "and don't you look lovely."

Joy smiled hello and said, "You look just the same as at the Algonquin, which is all one could ask. Do you know Mr. Masters? Mr. Kent, formerly of World Wide—Mr. Masters of Hollywood and allover."

Everybody knew Spookie Masters, the comedian, singer, dancer, dramatic actor and husband of beautiful women.

"Not personally," I said, shaking hands, "but I'm a longtime fan. How do you do."

"It's a pleasure, Kent," Masters said. "Joy tells me she's taken the vows and joined the Martians. I envy her. Their coming is probably the most exciting thing that's happened since. the wheel."

"They're a pretty lively bunch, all right," I said. "I don't know where it's all going to end, but it should be fun while it lasts."

"They sure beat the beatniks," Spookie Masters said, and I remembered that he'd been on a beatnik and bongo drums kick for a while. "I've got half a mind to take out a card myself. Who's the head alien, Joy? Where do I get the poop?"

"I think you're pulling my leg, Spookie," she said ("Love to," he said), "but if you're serious I'll speak to Frij. Just what is it you'd like to do?"

"Oh, just be an altar boy. Sit at the feet of the high priests and absorb their philosophy. I did that in Tibet once and I've never got over it. There's something more to life than chasing the old dollar. I've learned that much."

This Spookie Masters was a pretty charming guy. He was about forty, maybe five-feet-ten, and slender. Not handsome, but honest-faced.

A sort of cult had grown up around him. Spookie Masters was more than a million-a-year (net) entertainer. He was, to innumerable moviegoers and TV fans, a way of life. They'd followed his career from his beginning as a poor boy whose father had died in the electric chair. They knew about his several marriages to, and subsequent divorces from, some of the world's most glamorous women. They'd followed his rise to fame and plunge to obscurity and his comeback.

They knew about his coterie of big-name hangers-on, and they parroted the group's own special language. They marveled that his intimates and admirers included not only the mayor of a big city, the head of the philosophy department of an Ivy League university, the president of one of the world's biggest industries and the pretty sister of a reigning queen, but that he also had plenty of time for people who rode in subways and went to ball games and boxing matches. Spookie usually dressed like a prince, but when the whim took him he got into sport shirt, dungarees and sneakers and lounged through the streets, keeping in touch, as it were, with the life he'd known before fame struck. He'd browse in book stores, talk to panhandlers and sit in the bleachers and boo the Yankees. He had a man-next-door face and wasn't often recognized When he didn't want to be.

Spookie, Joy and I had wandered off the subject of the Monolithians and were discussing old movie stars when some-body banged a gong to get attention, then announced:

"Ladies and gentlemen, the President of the United States."

The deliberate aim at Peace very easily
passes into its bastard substitute,
Anaesthesia.
—Alfred North Whitehead

CHAPTER FIFTEEN
(AUG. 5, TUES.)

IT WAS about one o'clock in the morning. I'd called Mae
shortly after nine to tell her I was delayed and not to wait up for
me. The party apparently was still going strong, but diffused.
The Monolithians had provided a number of side rooms for
their guests to retire to from time to time to recuperate and
freshen up before returning for more food, drink and talk. It
was no Roman orgy—there were no beds in the rooms, for one
thing—but it gave every indication of lasting till dawn.

I was sitting with my feet up on a couch. I'd loosened my tie
and was drinking black coffee. I was beat.

Joy Linx came in. "Better start pulling yourself together.
The President wants to see you."

"Me? Now? Why?"

"He's in the mood, I guess," Joy said. "I am but the bearer
of the tidings. Are you sober?"

"Disgustingly," I said. "Where is he?"

"I'll take you there. Some party, eh, Sam?"

I couldn't agree that the party was in any way spectacular
except in length, so I merely grunted. It had been sort of fun
before President Allison arrived, and I'd enjoyed meeting
Spookie Masters. But after Gov got there it collapsed into a
formal gathering of anticipatory groups standing awkwardly and
waiting for the President to notice them. After an hour or so of
this I had fled to one of the recuperation rooms.

My face was a bit bristly with one o'clock shadow, but my tie
was back in place and I asked Joy if I looked presentable. She
ran her hand through my hair, presumably to tidy a cowlick, and

said, "You'll do nicely. Good luck, Sam. I hear he's very easy to talk to."

It was kind of her; I was feeling a bit nervous. I'd never had a great deal of respect, politically, for Gov Allison, but it's one thing to be a distant critic and another to be ushered into a Presence.

"Thanks," I said. "Which way?"

Joy led me down the hall and around a corner to a door outside which two men stood with seeming casualness. Secret Service, I supposed. They nodded and one of them opened the door for us when Joy said, "Mr. Sam Kent."

There was one other man in the room with the President. I recognized him as Rupert Marriner, the Secretary of State. Joy introduced me to Marriner, who introduced me to the President. Allison said, "How do you do," and I said something like, "It's a great pleasure, sir," and then Joy and Marriner left and I was alone with the President.

It was a medium-sized room equipped with a desk and straight chair, two easy chairs, a couch, a sideboard on which stood a big tray with bottles, glasses, an ice bucket and soda, a bookcase with sets of books uniformly bound (I noticed later that they were the complete works of Zane Grey and Edgar Wallace) and a Remington painting, or excellent reproduction, on the wall. Allison sat down in one of the easy chairs and invited me to take the other.

"Forgive the hour, Sam, but I wanted to see you here where we could have a private chat rather than in the White House for the first time, where there always seems to be something of an urgent nature coming up to take my attention and leaving me little time for the niceties, as I am sure you'll appreciate," the President said in one of his usual marathon sentences.

"Of course, sir," I said. "An excellent idea."

"First let me say this," he said: "There's no need to stand on formality with me in private. I'm a plain man, having been raised on a farm in Indiana and having mingled with all kinds in my calling, before politics, as a country lawyer. So when we're together alone—that is to say like now, in private—I want you to call me Gov. I've always been called Gov, though I never held the office of Governor, as you probably know (though I ran for it in, let me see, I think it Was 1948, and was pretty soundly beaten by that fellow what's-his-name), and Gov I want to be to my friends and associates except when the formalities of the occasion so decree. Will you go along with that, Sam? It will make us both more comfortable and engender a closer working arrangement, I feel."

"Yes, sir," I said. "That's fine—Gov." I felt thoroughly uncomfortable and hitched around in my chair. I wished I'd shaved. Allison himself looked spruce and freshly pressed, and his pink cheeks showed no trace of recent growth.

"Why don't we both have a drink, Sam?" Allison said.

"If you wouldn't mind pouring me a vodka and orange juice or something, and you have whatever you'd like, I think we'll break the ice a bit faster. I don't particularly like vodka, but a man in my job has to beware the breath of scandal, to coin a phrase, and I do mean breath."

He smiled, and I smiled back dutifully as I got up and went to the sideboard. I made him his orange blossom and took myself a healthy hooker of Scotch, with a bit of soda.

"Now we're relaxed," Allison said, smacking his lips over a big swallow. "It's good to kick your shoes off, so to speak, and settle down among friends. You're probably wondering how I happened to pick you for the job of press secretary. A natural curiosity. Let me say this, before I go any further: I've heard of you. Your work has, come to my attention now and again and of course I have an acquaintance with the Washington people on the staff of World Wide—McEachern and Sylvester among others. I know you to be a professional, and I think I can pay you no higher compliment."

The President paused for another swallow of his orange blossom and I said, "Thank you, sir."

"Gov," he said, smiling.

"Gov," I said. "Yes, sir."

"Naturally, when Josh was forced by the exigencies of the situation to bow out, I looked around for someone to fill his shoes. You were very highly recommended to me. I decided on the spot that you would be the man, without even having to see you. You're a smart lad and maybe you can guess who recommended you."

"The aliens?"

"Right the first time." Allison took a long swallow and handed me his empty glass. "If you don't mind."

I finished my own and went to the sideboard and made us two fresh ones. Vodka, in addition to being odorless, is supposed to be tasteless, so I gave Gov a double one, hoping he wouldn't notice and that he'd drop a few clues to the state of interplanetary affairs. I made my second Scotch a weak one.

"Here you are, Gov," I said, handing him his glass. I was getting into the groove.

"That's the stuff, Sammy boy," the President said. He'd probably had a few before he saw me. "Now, as I told you, I'm in the habit of speaking plainly. I see no reason to change that habit with you, here, now this minute, especially since one of your jobs, as press secretary, is to project the Presidential image the way people want it seen, regardless of what I really am."

The President took a long drink and went on. "You're a bright. boy, as I've mentioned, and you may have suspected the truth about me. Lots of people have, but, frankly, as long as the press goes on exercising its self-censorship and it doesn't come out in print until after I've gone—and that may not be too long now—I frankly don't give a damn. What I'm doing is coasting through my second term. Under the Constitution I can't be elected again, and let me tell you this: if anybody should propose re-amending it, I'll fight it."

"I think I know how you feel," I said, to give him time to take another drink.

"Of course you do," he said, having drunk. "Now let me go on. I've worked as hard as I had to for nearly six years, but now I'm tired. I'm 68 years old and there's never been a time in the last thirty years when I wasn't up to here in public office of one kind or another. It's a very tiring thing, that kind of responsibility, and I'm sick of it."

"I can understand that, sir," I said. I added quickly, "Gov."

"That's better," he said. He handed me his glass. "Not so much orange juice this time, Sam. Too much acid's bad for the system."

He went on talking while I fixed him his third drink. I decided to nurse mine along, though I went through the motions of freshening it.

"I've gathered a good team together," Allison said, "and from now on I'm going to let them do the work. They've been doing most of it anyhow. From now on I don't want to be bothered. I'll continue to make public appearances and sign the bills they don't want me to veto, but I'm damned if I'm going to aggravate my ulcers any more with problems. That's what you and the others are drawing your salaries for. It's enough, isn't it, what you're getting? Beats the World Wide pay scale, doesn't it? And that tax-free allowance is nice, too, isn't it?"

"Yes, sir," I said. "I've got no complaints, Gov."

"Good. That's your job then. Project the Presidential image and keep me off the hook. Do I make myself clear?"

"Absolutely. I understand perfectly." And don't let on, I added to myself, that the Monolithians are running things.

"Good. I'm sure I'm not shattering any of your illusions, as I said before. Every newsman worth his salt knows I've been easing off for the past year at least. I've reached the top. There's no place else to go. So I'm just going to sit in the big plush seat and try to enjoy it for the two years that are left. If I can last that out without busting a gut, I'll be seventy. Then maybe I can retire to a few more years of peace and quiet. Hire a ghost and sell my memoirs to *Life* for half a million or so. At any rate, from here on out it's all downhill for me, Monolithians or no Monolithians."

"I understand, Gov, and I certainly think you deserve a rest. I'll do everything I can." I didn't say what that everything would be.

"I'm sure you will. Let's have a nightcap now, and go easy on the orange juice. I don't know if you've been told, but I'll expect to see you in Washington in a couple of days. Somebody'll fix up a house for you. You have a wife, haven't you?"

"Yes. She's—we're going to be parents."

"Fine, fine. I'll see that they fix up the house with air-conditioning. That Washington climate is murder. You'll have a secretary, too. It's all been arranged. That Mix girl. She's in the picture."

"Linx," I said. "Joy Linx."

"She's the one. She doesn't know it yet. You can tell her if you like. About the secretaryship. She knows about the bigger picture, as I've mentioned." Allison leaned back and took a long swallow. "Any questions? Any at all?"

I decided it was time to say it. "The truth is, Gov, that the Monolithians are running things, isn't it?"

The President smiled. "I was afraid for a minute that I'd made a mistake. But I can see now that you're really the bright boy they say you are. You're right. The Monolithians are running it. And if you're as perceptive as I hope you are, you'll understand that this is the way it has to be." He paused, then added, "For now, anyway."

He took another swallow of his drink, looking at me over the top of his glass.

"One last thing," Gov said. "If you have any major questions or problems when I'm not handy, there's an old friend of mine who thinks very much the way I do. He'll be glad to advise you. He's Mr. Avery. Remember the name: Avery. Here's his telephone number." Gov passed me a slip of paper with a New York number on it. "But don't call him unless it's really important."

He finished his drink and set the glass down decisively. I took this to mean that the interview was at an end and got up.

"Yes, sir," I said, "good night, sir," intuitively reverting to formality. I had guessed correctly. He replied, "Good night, Kent. See you in the Big House."

The President had had a few, but I felt that his choice of words for the Executive Mansion was deliberate.

How many scruples in ten drams?
—The Complete Arithmetic, 1874

CHAPTER SIXTEEN
(AUG. 6, WED.)

MAE DIDN'T want to fly, so we left early and drove down to Washington. This made it possible to avoid whatever kind of official airport reception might have been arranged for me. We went right to our new house in Bethesda.

It was a beautiful little house, in a wooded section, and air-conditioned, as Gov had promised. The phone was in and Mae called Ann McEachern, Ian's wife, who had said she'd come over from Silver Spring as soon as we got in. Ann was there in half an hour and I left for the National Press Building. I wanted to see Ian and read the news before I checked in at the White House.

Reb Sylvester was on the desk and Ian had just got back from lunch. "Well, well," Ian said, "if it isn't Mr. Kent, back to see his old cronies. Congratulations, Sam."

"Thanks. But what's going on here?" The office was a mess. There was paper allover the floor and tags on the filing cabinets.

"We're moving—haven't you heard? *They're* moving, that is. I quit this morning."

"What do you mean quit? Did you get drafted, too?"

"No such luck, if luck is the word I want. I just resigned. Tomorrow I start making the rounds to see if they need anybody at the AP or Reuters or the *Times.*"

"Look, Ian," I said. "This is all too fast for me. How about going up to the Press Club and telling me about it over a drink?"

"Okay," he said, after the slightest of hesitations. "For old times' sake, okay."

Reb said as we went out, "Have one for me. I need it."

We ordered rum-and-cokes at the bar and I asked Ian, "Is Reb leaving, too?"

"He doesn't know what he's going to do yet. It's all happened pretty fast. One minute we're up there with the world's top news services and the next minute we're a government mouthpiece."

"You mean World Wide sold out?"

"Lock, stock and teletypes. It was one of those top-level decisions. Nobody knew about it till it was all over."

"But why?" I asked him. "They've got the Voice of America. What do they want with another propaganda outfit?"

"The way I see it, they want to propagandize the Americans. The Voice only goes overseas. Besides, it always takes a while for the facts to get around. In the meantime they'll have got their message across. By God, Sam, if I'd wanted to be a flack for somebody I'd have gone into P.R., and that nice money, a long time ago."

I took a slug of my rum coke and asked, "Where are they moving to? I don't see why they have to move at all."

Ian swallowed the rest of his drink and ordered two more. "I'm surprised you hadn't heard. Since you don't know, this will give you a laugh. World Wide is moving into the White House."

"The White House?"

"That's what I said. You'll be right at home. Door A, Executive Mansion, the President. Door B, his press agent, Sam Kent. Door C, World Wide. Nice, huh? Bye-bye free press." He took his new drink. "Bye-bye Constitution. I give you a toast, friend: Here's mud in the eye of the Bill of Rights."

I didn't drink. Neither did Ian.

"Well," I said.

"And well may you say 'Well,'" said Ian. "A pretty stinking kettle of fish, you might say."

I tried to look at it another way. "Maybe it's not so bad. Look at France Presse. That's government-subsidized."

"This isn't France," Ian said. "We happen to do things differently here."

"Vive l'Amérique," I said. "Once upon a time, eh?"

I toyed with a pretzel from a bowl on the bar. Ian watched me and said, "That pretzel is as straight as a string compared with what's been going on in the last couple of weeks." He picked up a pretzel of his own and bit it in two. "That is, if you want my opinion, Mr. Press Secretary."

I had always valued the opinion of Ian McEachern and I told him so. "I don't like it," I said. "I don't like it at all. But what can we do? I mean what can I do? You've already done it—you've quit, honest journeyman journalist that you are. But what can I do?"

"Don't laugh at my principles," Ian said. "They happen to be sincere."

"I wasn't laughing, Ian." I felt like patting him on the shoulder, but thought better of it. I swallowed half my drink instead. "I admire your integrity," I said, then took the sincerity out of it by adding, "if I can make such a statement in the bar of the National Press Club."

"Are you laughing at me again?" Ian looked hurt and I became absolutely sober.

"Ian," I said, "whatever happens, believe this: you're one of my favorite people. I'm just not in a position now to be as straightforward as you are. I just can't explain, but I want you to know that I haven't sold out to the aliens, and..."

Ian looked surprised. "I never thought you had. For heaven's sake, man, I haven't questioned your patriotism!"

He hadn't, of course. He didn't know all that I knew about the invisible links between the Monolithians and the President.

Suddenly I felt like getting very drunk. "Two more," I said to the bartender. To Ian I said, "You certainly, don't owe anything to World Wide. You don't have to go back, do you? Let's get loaded, then get a bottle and go home to Mae and Ann and start all over again."

Ian solemnly finished his old drink. "Sam," he said, "you've had some great ideas in the past, but I am prepared to say that this is the greatest. Bartender, two more."

"I've already ordered two."

"Yes," Ian said. "But two and two make four. I still know that much. Drink up."

"When they don't make five," I said. "I already did. Finish yours and have a pretzel."

He picked up one of the twisted, baked, salted pieces of dough and looked at it critically. "It's an honest piece of work," Ian said. "I now perceive its simple integrity. I shall eat a bowlful while I get drunk with you. Forgive me, pretzel, while I consume you."

Inwardly pretzel-like, I forgave him and proceeded to drink a large number of rum cokes.

Every day, in every way, I am getting
better and better.
—Émile Coué

CHAPTER SEVENTEEN
(AUG. 7, THURS.)

I HAD ONE of those heartbeat hangovers where every
pump of blood sent a hammer of pain to my head.

Mae was being very good and gave me coffee and eggs and
tomato juice and aspirin, and I managed to shower and shave
under my own power.

An expense-account taxi took me downtown to the White
House. The guards at the gate glanced at my identification and
waved me on. It should have been a proud moment—my first
day on the job in the Executive Mansion—but I felt like. hell.
It wasn't only the hangover, which had begun to recede to a dull
throb. It was the disenchantment with the whole picture.
Instead of walking in with head high I sort of shuffled in,
looking at my feet, and almost bumped into a man in the lobby.

It was Rod Harris of the AP. I'd never met him but I knew
him by sight. If there was anybody I didn't want to see right this
minute it was a representative of the free and untrammeled
press.

"You're Sam Kent, aren't you?" Rod said, introducing
himself. I gave him a hearty but phony handshake and said, "I
hope you haven't got sixteen questions to throw at me all at
once. I'd appreciate it if you'd give me a chance to find my way
around first."

"Sure," Rod said. "No hurry at all. I just wanted to say
congratulations, on behalf of the White House Correspondents
Association."

"That's very nice of you. Thanks. I appreciate it."

"One thing, though," Rod said. "I might as well say it and
get it over with. We held a meeting last night and voted to drop
World Wide from membership. Nothing personal, and we were

sorry as hell to have to do it, but—well, I think you understand."

"Oh?" I said. "You did, eh? Well, I'm sorry to hear that. But Ian beat you to it and quit."

"I know. Ian's one of the best. It's rough on him. It's also rough on Stew Macon. World Wide rushed him down here to replace Ian and he's wandering around like a dog with skunk-smell all over him, poor guy."

"Stew? Where is he?"

"He's in your office."

"I'd better go cheer him up. Look, I'll see you and the other guys later. Josh used to hold his daily briefings about eleven, didn't he? I'll try to have something for you then."

"Okay," Rod said. "Good luck."

"Thanks." I didn't say I'd need it, but I sure thought it.

I knew where the Press Secretary's office was from earlier junkets to Washington. I went in and found Stew pacing up and down the room, smoking.

"Hi, chiefie," he said. "Boy, am I glad to see you. I feel like a pariah."

"Misery loves company, eh?"

"You can say that again. Boy, do you look terrible. Aren't you happy here in the old lap of the gods?"

"Happy as the ninth pup at feeding time," I said. "I spent the night getting drunk with your predecessor and I've got the grandfather of all hangovers."

"Poor Ian," Stew said. He sat on the big desk that was now mine and put his cigarette out in an oversized ashtray. "Poor me, too. I thought this was gong to be a big deal, taking over the Washington bureau. John Hyatt told me Ian quit, but he didn't tell me why. I thought my biggest problem was going to be getting along with Reb Sylvester, who must have figured he was in line for bureau chief. But this is another kettle entirely."

"I suppose you're *persona non grata* in the press room?"

"The chill is on, believe me. Continental's in the same boat. But their man didn't even show up this morning."

Ian had mentioned that Continental Broadcasting Corporation had also been bought up.

"Look," I said. "You don't have to go back to the press room. Ian said last night WW's moved into the White House. All we have to do is find Door C. That's where he said it is. Let me ring the old bell and find out where Door C is."

"I'd rather be in the press room," Stew said, but I found a button and pressed it.

"Yes, Mr. Kent?" a woman's voice said.

"Where's Door C?"

"I beg your pardon?" The voice sounded vaguely familiar.

"Where is World Wide?"

"Oh, it's just on the other side of your office, Mr. Kent. I'll be glad to show you."

"Good."

One of my three doors opened and Joy Linx came in. "Good morning, Sam," she said.

"Well, good morning," I said. "What are you doing here?" Then I remembered that Gov had said she'd be with me in Washington.

"I'm your secretary," Joy said. "I thought they told you."

"They did and I'm delighted," I said. "Forgive me for not remembering. I'll need every friendly face there is. Joy, I want you to meet another fly in the web—Stew Macon. Stew, this is Joy Linx, somebody's Girl Friday. I guess now she's mine."

"Some people have all the luck," Stew said. "Hi, Joy. I'm delighted, too."

"Now for that door," Joy said. She opened the third door and said, "Behold, World Wide."

It was virtually a duplicate of World Wide's New York newsroom. There were the banks of teletype and the piles of newspapers and the desks. Reb Sylvester sat in the slot, a cup of coffee on the desk next to a row of freshly sharpened pencils. He was smoking a pipe and reading the comic page of the *Washington Post*.

"What's new, Reb?" I said.

He put down the paper. "Funny you should ask that, Sam," he said. "Nothing is. It's absolutely dead. Have you got a dispatch, perchance?"

"Hi, Reb," Stew said.

"Hi, Stew. What's happening at the crossroads of the free world? What's the true poop? Are there any bulletins or flashes to be sent this humid forenoon?"

Reb was obviously in a bitter mood. He'd been passed over for promotion, not to mention being sold out.

"What's on the wire so far?" I asked him.

"Out of Washington? Well, we've got a hundred words on the little girl who was mauled by the lion in the zoo and a fifty-word follow-up on the woman who had quadruplets yesterday. Aside from that it's been rather quiet. At the moment we're waiting, you might say, for the morning briefing by the Presidential Press Secretary to learn whether our proud Ship of State is still afloat."

This was a boy who needed stepping on. Or else he was a thoroughly disillusioned reporter masking his true feelings with quips.

I gave him the benefit of the doubt and said, "The old ship has survived a lot worse than this. As for the other, I'll be seeing Gov in a little while. That might produce a little news."

Stew said, "See you later, then. I'll stay here and try out the typewriters."

My hangover was waking up again and I was glad to get out of the newsroom and back to my own office. Joy Lime was waiting for me with an Alka-Seltzer and a cup of coffee.

"Thanks, Joy. How'd you know?"

"It's my job to know, Mr. Kent."

"Cut out that Mr. Kent stuff. I'm just old Sam, the confused man. What do you know about all these new goings-on?"

"Which new goings-on in particular? There've been a whole passel of them."

"Oh, there have, have there? Tell me about World Wide and Continental for a starter."

"It all ties in with the big picture," Joy said. "We want the Americans to have the true official position when the big stories break."

"Who's we? And why couldn't the free press be depended on to give the true story? It always has."

"*We* is the government, of course. As for the other, I think it has to do with point of view. The facts have a way of being misinterpreted by a hostile press."

"Oh, and it'll be the job of World Wide and Continental to spoon-feed the official line down the public's throat?"

"That's a rather crude way to put it, but I'd say it's accurate. We've hired Clyde B. Fitchburn to help."

"What?" I said. "Not the Voice of Doom?"

Joy smiled. "The same. We couldn't afford to have him on the other side, spreading hysteria. So he's been persuaded to join up."

"It's amazing," I said, "what a lot of money will do."

"Don't be cynical, Sam."

Joy said no more than that. She didn't have to. As a dweller myself in a big glass house I was especially vulnerable to rocks. I took a contrite swallow of coffee and said, "Okay. We'll ease away from that one. Now what are the big stories? It seems to me that I'm the least-informed Press Secretary of all time."

"Well, there's the summit conference," Joy said. She couldn't have been more off-hand about it if she had said, "It's ten o'clock."

"*What* summit conference?" I practically yelled. "When?" Where?"

"I'll start with *who,*" Joy said. "It'll be the heads of government of the United States, the Soviet Union, Britain, France, Germany, India, Israel, the United Arab Republic, Japan and China. Both Chinas. I think that's all. Oh, and the Secretary-General of the United Nations and the Monolithians, of course."

"Of course," I said, dazed. "And when is this little huddle taking place? It's bound to take months of preparation."

"Not at all. It's scheduled for Saturday."

"Saturday! Not *this* Saturday? The day after tomorrow?"

"That's right. Saturday, August ninth."

"You'd better make me another Alka-Seltzer."

"Okay," she said. "That'll give you a chance to brace your-self for the *where.*"

I poured down the fizzing drink and felt it start to work in my poor stomach.

"I guess I'm ready now. Where is this crazy summit conference going to be held? Here? London? Moscow? If it's here I'm going to cut my throat right now. It's bad enough covering such a free-for-all, it'll be murder organizing it."

"Put your razor away," Joy said. "It's not going to be held here. It's going to be held in space."

The President buzzed for me while I was still trying to take it all in. He was very businesslike, with none of the man-to-man intimacy of the other night. He welcomed me to the job, said he assumed Miss Linx had filled me in on the summit conference and told me he wanted me to make the announcement at my 11 o'clock press briefing. He handed me a prepared statement that he said was being issued more or less simultaneously in London, Moscow, Cairo, Paris and all the other capitals concerned.

Gov looked tired. I tried to question him but he said most of the answers were in the statement, which ran to about 600 words. Everything else was off the record and I'd have to say, "no comment."

As for himself, he was not going to hold a press conference this week and there probably wouldn't be any other news until after everybody got back from Ultra.

"Ultra?" I asked.

"That's the name of the space station where we'll be meeting. The Monolithians moored it out there in whatever the hell it's called—cislunar space. This side of the moon. It's in the handout."

"Yes, sir," I said, glancing through it quickly. "When will you be leaving?"

"Tomorrow morning, but that's off the record. You'll be going, too, Sam, and so will Miss Linx, so you'd better pack an overnight bag."

My reaction to that must have shown in my face, because the President said, "I'm not looking forward to the trip, either, Sam, but it has to be made and we might as well reconcile ourselves to getting it over with. Everything ought to be a lot simpler afterward."

I was curious to know what hidden meaning, if any, there was in that last remark, but he waved me out.

My first meeting with the press, which I had been dreading, went off beautifully. Any personal or sarcastic questions the reporters might have asked were forgotten as I made the summit-in-space announcement and passed the handout around. I answered a few questions without going beyond the words of the announcement, but then, on being pressed, I made up a headline phrase to summarize the purpose of the precedent-shattering conclave. Its aim, I said, cribbing a bit from the Constitution, was to secure the blessings of interplanetary peace, friendship and liberty. Actually, that was what the 600-word statement added up to, more or less.

Just before they began their mad dash to the telephones I told them the lid was on—that there'd be nothing further from the White House today.

Joy closed the door behind the last of them and I collapsed into my chair. She gave me a sympathetic smile.

"So much for that," she said. "I think it went very well. Now is it time to lock up the shop and pack for our space journey?"

The old keyboard test, designed to cover all contingencies, came to my mind. "Pack my bag with six dozen liquor jugs," I said. "And maybe that wouldn't be a bad idea."

> They did not see it until the atomic
> bombs burst in their fumbling hands.
> —H. G. Wells, 1914

CHAPTER EIGHTEEN
(AUG. 8, FRI.)

MAE HAD HEARD the news on the radio and TV, of course, and she was pretty well prepared for what I had to tell her—that I was going off into space with the world's big wheels. Naturally she didn't like it, but for a reason I hadn't suspected. She told me about it in the morning over my Pep and eggs.

"It seems to me, Sam, that you've been acting very peculiar ever since you took this new job. And I don't just mean your worry about your new responsibilities. I can understand that. What I don't understand is why you've become so cool towards me."

"Why, honey!" I said, really surprised. "That's not so at all."

"Oh, isn't it! I get the impression that I'm being taken for granted; that I'm supposed to be satisfied with a little pat on the head now and again while you cavort around with your high and mighty new friends. You never take me anywhere any more. Why? Is it because I'm so ugly—so—so—misshapen?"

"Mae!" I was shocked. "Now you cut that right out!"

"Well, sometimes I wonder. Then there's that Linx girl. You never told me about her—and you should have, if there's nothing to hide."

"For heaven's sake, Mae," I said. "Of course there's nothing to hide. Why, you're jealous, aren't you?"

"Certainly I'm jealous. Is that so strange? It isn't as if you'd been honest with me and said there was this girl, but that I'm prettier in spite of my condition—"

"Now, Mae," I said. "You are prettier—and it's *because* of your condition. Who told you about Joy anyway? I'll bet it was that Ann McEachern—she's jealous herself because I've got a good job and her Ian's temporarily out of work. There's nothing about Joy, any more than there is to tell about my three telephones. I never had three telephones before, either."

"Well…" Mae said. "If you're sure."

"Sure I'm sure. Now you just stop worrying your pretty head about stupid nonsense like that and give me a kiss goodbye. I'll be back by Sunday or Monday." I picked up my bag.

"All right," she said. "I'm sorry. I don't want you to go, but I know you have to. And I feel better knowing *she* won't be going, either."

I put the bag down again.

"Mae," I said. "Listen, Mae."

She burst into tears.

"Now, Mae!"

"She *is* going!" Mae sobbed. "Oh-h-h!"

"Yes, she is. And so is the President, and so are several prime ministers and premiers and that imbecile Addison Madison and Mox and protocol officers and the Secretary-General and a whole gaggle of Monolithians. For Pete's sake, Mae! This is probably the most important conference ever held in the history of man, not a weekend at Atlantic City!"

It took me half an hour to calm her down and get away. I was much lower in my mind by then and not at all convinced that Mae understood, though she had put on a brave face.

Joy, the object of my wife's concern, was waiting for me at the office with a new crisis.

"Sam," she said, "I tried to get you at home, but you'd left."

"You mean you talked to Mae?"

"Yes. She's sweet. We had a nice chat."

I groaned. "You'd better get her back for me. Never mind; I'll get her later. What's the matter?"

"The press is coming, too."

"That's impossible! We'd have to take at least one from every country represented. There isn't room."

"Yes there is. The Monolithians provided another ship. I've got the list drawn up. All you have to do is check it over."

"All right. Let me see it."

They were all there: AP and UPI, representing a North American press pool; radio and TV men, magazine writers, Reuters; France Presse, Tass, Press Trust of India, New China News and so forth. Somebody had exerted the influence of the host country and worked in such supernumeraries as the Voice of America, World Wide, Continental Broadcasting and our old friend Clyde B. Fitchburn. I was glad to see Stew Macon's name next to WW's.

"Fine," I said, initialing the list and handing it back to Joy. "When do we leave? Same time?"

"Yes. Noon by helicopter from the back lawn."

"Good. You all ready yourself, Joy?"

"Yop. Got my toothbrush, wash-'n'-dry undies and spare lipstick." She gave me a wink I didn't entirely fathom and went into her own office, saying, "Better call your wife, now."

I dialed our Bethesda number and talked to Mae for about five minutes. You can say a lot in that time, but for the life of me all I could remember of Mae's conversation was, "I love you and I know you love me. I'm sorry I made that fuss about Joy Linx. We had a nice chat. I think she's sweet."

I went out to the helicopter a very confused man.

At Andrews Air Force Base in Maryland we transferred from the helicopter to two space ships. The helicopters had been jam-packed, but there was room to spare on the ships.

I had a cabin next to the President's suite, and Joy's was next to mine. World Wide, the Voice of America and Continental shared one across the corridor, but the AP, Reuters and the other independent agencies were on the second ship, fuming, I'm sure, at the discrimination—especially since the British, French and German summitters were on ours. Presumably there was going to be a sort of sub-summit conference en route.

I had a big question that I wanted answered before the press got at me and, as soon as we were settled, I knocked at the President's door.

"Come in," Gov said. "Oh, hello, Sam. What's up?"

I asked my question: "Who represents the Monolithians?"

"Shut the door, Sam, and sit down. I can answer that several ways. One, by saying they all represent each other, like bees in a hive or ants in a hill—a sort of group intelligence with nobody's thinking very far out of line from anybody else's. Two, by saying their big wheel at the moment is that Addison Madison, or Frij, fellow, a more insulting parody of an American Earthman than I could have imagined possible. Three, by saying I haven't the faintest idea who they'll produce when they get us to Ultra—quite possibly someone who's never been to Earth at all. Any other questions?"

"Yes, sir, if you don't mind. What are you and the Big Three Europeans going to discuss before you get to Ultra?"

"I frankly don't know, son, but I can make a guess. We'll probably have a few drinks and talk about the good old days when all we had to worry about was the Russian or the Chinese menace."

I started to interrupt, but Gov held up a hand. "I know you can't put that in a communiqué. All-right, you can say we had a frank and wide-ranging exchange of views and vowed to take any steps, consistent with honor, that would advance the cause of international and interplanetary peace. That ought to be diplomatic and obfuscatory enough for anybody."

I grinned. "Yes, sir. The cast may change, but never the language."

Gov smiled back, but with an effort.

"Better get back to your cabin now and batten down," he said. "I understand a Monolithian blast-off is a lot kinder to the kidneys than anything our astronauts had to go through, but it's still no bed of nasturtiums. The things they expect an old boy to put up with for his country…I'm glad I've taken my last oath of office."

I left the President settling down into his padded couch and went to my own.

The blast-off was a short nightmare of vibration and pressure. Then it was over. There was a moment of nauseous weightlessness before the artificial gravity took hold and a soothing chime sounded which, we'd been told, meant we could get up and move about normally.

My door opened and Stew Macon started to come in. He changed his mind when he saw the British Prime Minister, the French President and the German Chancellor go by on their way to Gov's suite. But Stew was back soon.

"They won't talk," he said. "I didn't really think they would."

"Never mind," I told him. "I've got it all here."

"What they're going to say?"

"What they will have officially said. It's not very much."

"Let me have it now. I'll put it out under embargo."

"No you won't. You'll get it after they come out and I've radioed it to the boys in the other ship. I don't want them any sorer at us than they are already."

Stew looked hurt. "I thought we were pals."

"Pals-schmals, this is official business. Why don't you go; up to the bridge and see who's driving? That ought to make a dandy feature."

"Continental's doing that on tape. They're going to fill me in later."

"What's the Voice doing?"

"Rehashing the AP and Reuters," Stew said disgustedly. "I tell you, this being subsidized is for the birds. You're further away from the news than anybody else."

"True," I said. "And if I were still with WW I'd complain."

"Yeah? To who?"

"To the Presidential Press Secretary, for instance."

"That's you. A big help you are."

"Them's the conditions that prevail."

"Funny man," Stew said. "Jimmy Durante."

There was a knock on my door and Joy Linx came in.

"Hello, men," she said. "How are the old space voyagers?"

"Nuts," Stew said. "I've had bigger thrills on the Staten Island ferry."

"Sam, I've got the radioteletype set up for the communiqué. Want to check it out?"

"Sure." We all went into her office-cabin.

"Just the one machine," Joy said. "The press ship is tuned in and drop copies go to WW, Continental and the Voice here."

"Fine." I sat down and typed:

KENT HERE. TESTING.

The reply was: WHIRLPOOL HERE. GA.

"Whirlpool?" I asked Joy. "What have they got, a sponsor?"

She laughed. "It's their code name. It stands for World Press Pool."

"Oh." I typed:

WESTERN BIG FOUR BEGAN SHIPBOARD SUBSUM-MIT TALKS AT 1607 EDT. EXPECT TO HAVE BRIEF COMMUNIQUE SOON. ALL FOR NOW.

ROGER, the reply came: OVER AND OUT.

"Incurious bunch," Stew said. "Don't they have any questions?"

"I guess they prefer not to be confused by our meager facts. Makes it easier for them to interview each other and bat out learned think-pieces."

The Western Big Four ended their conference, or whatever it was, and Gov called me to say I could release the communiqué. I tried to get him to elaborate on it, or at least tell me off the record what they'd really discussed, but he refused. Gov sounded tired and irritable.

I put the communiqué on the teletype to the other ship and told them there was nothing else at the moment. Again there was a surprising lack of curiosity from the free press. They asked a couple of routine questions and I answered them and shut down the machine. I was beginning to feel rebuked and useless.

"Do they have a bar on this boat?" I asked Joy, who was filing away a copy of the uninformative communiqué in. an impressive leather-bound folder labeled in gold: MONOLITHIA-ULTRA.

"Well now," she said, "I'm glad you asked me that question. Yes, as a matter of fact. And would you be after offering to buy me a drink?"

"I most delightedly would," I said. "Or two or three."

Relaxed now at the bar, with Joy on the stool beside me and a tall drink on the mahogany, I had time to think.

Joy said, "A penny for your thoughts."

I roused myself from my reverie and said, "I was just wondering what's going to be the outcome of all this."

"A good wonder," she said. "I guess it's worth a penny. Frankly, I don't worry much about it. Assuming, of course, that we all come through it with our health, happiness and honor intact."

The Monolithian bartender was in front of us suddenly. He smiled.

There was a snort from our right. It was a man of about sixty who was drinking a Pernod.

"Ah, a philosopher," Joy said.

The man picked up his drink, admired its cloudy color and took a sip before replying. "I am indeed," he said. "My eyes are wide open and unfilmed."

"*Whose* eyes?" I said.

"Mine—the eyes of Clyde B. Fitchburn, student of men."

"Fitchburn!" I said. "The renowned crier of doom?"

"The *former* crier of doom," he said placidly. "Student of men and current employee of Monolithia. My cries are stilled while I remain on the payroll. What's your excuse, Mr. Kent? And yours, Miss Linx?"

I didn't like his tone. "Now look—" I started to say, but Joy put her hand on my arm.

"He's got a point," she said. "Aren't we all on the payroll?"

I had to admit in my secret mind that this was a valid point. And I said, "Let's leave us out of it. We don't matter, except to ourselves—"

"Oh, but we do," Fitchburn said. "We matter in direct ratio to the millions, or thousands, or even one that we influence. But go on, Kent."

He was an irritating man because he was speaking the truth—perhaps for the first time in his life.

"All right," I said angrily. "We matter to some extent. I grant you that—and that influence on one person, rightly exerted, can change the course of empire. But our influence is insignificant compared with that of the big boys. And we've got the biggest boys in the world aboard. What's *their* excuse?"

Clyde B. Fitchburn took out a crushable pack and lit a thinking-man's cigarette. The bartender rushed over to light it for him.

"Thank you," Fitchburn said to the Monolithian. "Listen if you like. I know you will anyway."

The bartender smiled and deliberately went to the other end of the bar. I was sure he could hear just as well from there.

Fitchburn turned back to Joy and me. "Each of us has his own secret soul," he said, and punctuated that profound remark with a sip of Pernod. "I took this job, which entailed an end to my well-known destructive criticism of the administration, because my third wife has gone into court with a demand for more alimony. For me it's as simple as that. I can fight the demand with lawyers, or I can pay. Either way I need more money. You, Miss Linx, took your job because you saw a possibility of meeting more important people and thus advancing your career—or alternatively, meeting more interesting people and perhaps finding an intelligent and well-to-do mate. Am I not right, my dear?"

"Look, Joy," I said, "we don't have to sit here and listen to this—"

"Simmer down, Sam," she said. "Mr. Fitchburn's honesty is refreshing, if not altogether flattering. Mr. Fitchburn—may I call you Clyde?"

"Please do."

"Clyde," she said, "I admire you. Frankly, I always dialed you out when I accidentally heard you on the air. It's a pity more people can't hear you over a drink, without benefit of microphone. A frank question, Clyde: What do you now consider your role to be?"

"An easy question from a friend," Fitchburn said. "I am, as of 48 hours ago, approximately, an apologist for the well-paying Monolithians. And you, Miss Linx?"

"Joy," she said. "A fearful Joy, perhaps, to steal the words of Mr. Cary, but an honest one, I hope. My role? You've already said it, Clyde. Meeting interesting, friendly people, with a loving but calculating female eye to the future. There—now I've said it, too."

"But what do you fear?" Fitchburn asked.

"That the Monolithians are not all they profess to be. That their humanity—their seeming friendliness to us Earthpeople—is motivated by something we don't know anything about. That in the end we're all going to be more miserable for it—if we exist to be miserable at all."

I ate a pretzel, feeling like a supernumerary carrying a rubber-tipped spear. I ate several pretzels, moodily, recalling my experience in the spaceship in the woods, my imprisonment and brain-picking and the covey of doubles for famous personages. And who were those aboard this spaceship? The real articles or the Monolithian duplicates?

"You'll get fat, eating all those pretzels," Joy said.

Clyde had said something to her and she to him and now she was worried about me. I was worried about me, too, and it had nothing to do with pretzels. It had to do with the whole human race.

"How well do you know President Allison?" I asked Clyde.

"As well as any reporter does," he said. "Maybe better—I had a private interview with him about a year ago."

"And the British Prime Minister? And the Frenchman and the German?"

"Slightly. I've met them at receptions a few times. Why?"

"Have you talked to them since they came aboard?"

"Yes. Not long. Just to say hello. What are you getting at, Kent?"

"I'm not sure. Did they look all right to you?"

"They all seemed weary and irritable, but otherwise okay. Two of them even remembered my name, which is a damn good average."

"What's this all about, Sam?" Joy asked. "You sound as if you have some inside information."

"I do," I said. "But I wonder what good it does me. It's something like a movie you've seen before. You know how it's going to end and there's no way to change it."

"My, you're morbid," Joy said. "I hope your movie had a happy ending."

Clyde Fitchburn had been gazing into his Pernod. "I've been thinking," he said to Joy. "The things our young friend here has been saying—or hinting—are beginning to tie in. I did notice something about our VIP's. Yes, definitely, now that I think of it. They looked tired, as I said. But that other thing I noticed—as I think back, it seems to me it wasn't just irritation. No; they were frightened. Yes, that's the word. Frightened. Scared to death."

"You mean they were afraid of this trip?" Joy asked. "I can't blame them for that. I'm still a little queasy after that takeoff. Little old internal organs may never be the same."

"Not that," Clyde said. "There was nothing cowardly about their fear. I know I'm expressing this badly, but it seemed to me that their trepidation was not for themselves—they're bigger men than that. No, it was as if there were something they were being forced to do—something that each had decided for himself had to be done. Each had made this great decision he could not avoid. It had to be made and each knew it was as right as any decision he had *ever* made. But having made it, he wasn't sure the next step, which was out of his hands, would be the right one. Each of them—yes, I'm convinced of it now—was frightened for all humanity."

The bartender came over and said, "You are all very amusing, but while you have been libeling the Monolithians, one of your Earth nations has begun a war against the rest of your unhappy planet."

"What?" I said. "Which one?"

"What do you mean?" Joy asked. "How?"

Clyde Fitchburn merely twirled his glass in his hand and smiled sadly.

"You would not suspect. A tiny Caribbean country. The one ruled by that man with the big mouth. I believe it's called El Spaniola."

The fack can't be no longer disguised
that a Krysis is onto us.
—Artemus Ward

CHAPTER NINETEEN
(AUG. 9, SAT.)

THE STORY was coming in on the teletypes.

LA PLAZA, EL SPANIOLA. Aug. 9 (AP)—El Spaniola's military overlord, General Rafael Domingo Sanchez, today warned mankind that an O-bomb is poised, ready to drop, over each of the world's major cities. Unless there is unconditional surrender by noon (EST) today, he declared, they will be blasted into oblivion.

The ultimatum from this tiny Caribbean island nation, until last night dependent on its coffee and banana crops for its livelihood, specifically mentioned New York, London, Moscow, Peking, Paris, Bonn, Rio de Janeiro, Melbourne, Tokyo and Bombay. It cautioned, however, that the omission of any city from the list did not necessarily mean that it was not also threatened.

El Spaniola, which has over the past 18 months been secretly buying long range jetliners and converting them to bombers, claimed also to have given asylum to Dr. Franz Kuperman, the convicted atomic spy who disappeared after serving a ten-year term in a U.S. federal prison…

HAVANA, Aug. 9 (UPI)—The secret of the A-bomb, which today threatens the extinction of the planet, is a simple one which spymaster Franz Kuperman took into Spaniolan exile with him, diplomatic sources here said today. The scientists of the Western and Soviet worlds were frantically working toward that secret when Kuperman made his knowledge and its resulting power available to the four million population banana-and-coffee "republic" of El Spaniola. Looming large…

PARIS, Aug. 9 (AFP)—The absence today of the world's leading statesmen, now on the Monolithian satellite of Ultra, made it doubtful that there would be a quick reply from the Quai D'Orsay to the threat of El Spaniola.

"We must await word from our President," a spokesman said at 6 A.M. (EST). "He is undoubtedly in consultation with our allies and, at this very moment, charting a course of action."

LONDON, Aug. 9 (Reuters)—The Foreign Office had no immediate comment early today on the bomb threat alleged to be poised over London and other world capitals.

The acting prime minister urged the nation to be calm. He said he did not entirely discount the possibility that the threat was a hoax or a bluff, although radar did confirm that an unidentified aircraft was circling high overhead.

As a precaution the Air Ministry ordered all planes, civil and military, grounded.

WASHINGTON, Aug. 9 (WW)—The question of why El Spaniola's A-bombers can't be shot out of the air was answered today by Pentagon sources. Each of the terrible bombs is encased in a virtually indestructible shell and cannot be detonated by another explosion. Thus, even though the bomber were to be pulverized, the O-bomb itself would survive and fall toward its target, exploding at a prearranged altitude chosen to achieve maximum destruction...

BULLETIN

SOMEWHERE IN CISLUNAR SPACE, Aug. 9 (AP)—A giant spaceship carrying the leaders of Earth to a historic conference made contact today with the Monolithian satellite Ultra, but the talks were overshadowed by El Spaniola's threatened destruction of major world centers...

BULLETIN

ABOARD THE SATELLITE ULTRA, Aug. 9 (UPI)—Monolithia assured the world today that no harm would come to any of its cities despite the O-bomb ultimatum of El Spaniola.

The assurance came in a joint communiqué issued by Earth's major nations and the United Nations Secretary-General, Nils Nilsen.

They said they were supremely confident, on the basis of what the Monolithians had told them, that no O-bomb would be dropped and that El Spaniola would be justly dealt with for its threat to the peace of the world.

While it was not explicitly stated in the communiqué, it was understood that the superior science of the Monolithians was more than sufficient to disarm or render harmless the Spaniolan O-bombers.

The text of the communiqué was...

ULTRA, Aug. 9 (AP)—The abortive attempt of El Spaniola to seize world domination during the absence from Earth of the world's leaders was seen here as a warning to any would-be dictator that he would get nowhere fast.

BULLETIN

LA PLAZA, EL SPANIOLA, Aug. 9 (UPI)—Rafael Domingo Sanchez, El Spaniola's strong man, bowed to a Monolithian edict today and ordered his dozen or more O-bombers to return home from around the world, their death-dealing weapons undropped. He sent word out from his fortress palace that there would be no explanation from him of what threat or persuasion the Monolithians had used to thwart his plan for world conquest...

HAVANA, Aug. 9 (AFP)—Rumors circulated here today that a "conscience gas" was the secret Monolithian weapon that had forced the Spaniolan dictator, Domingo Sanchez, to call off his threat to wipe out a big percentage of the world's population.

NEW YORK, Aug. 9 (Tass)—Reports that "conscience gas" had been used by the extraterrestrials to abort the Spaniolan threat to humanity were greeted with dismay in Wall Street circles today.

Financial and big business tycoons were said to be shuddering in their expensive shoes for fear that the gas might also be used against them.

The capitalist chiefs were reported to have hurriedly arranged a conference with their captive Congressmen to have them introduce legislation to prohibit the use of any such gas. They feared, of course, that if they were exposed to its effects— perhaps at the bargaining table with representatives of organized labor—their ability to exploit the workers for fantastic profits would be at an end. The whole capitalistic hierarchy...

Me seemes the world is runne quite out of square,
From the first point of his appointed sourse,
And being once amisse growes daily wourse and wourse.
—Edmund Spenser

CHAPTER TWENTY
(AUG. 10. SUN.)

"DON'T BOTHER ME," I said, pulling the sheet back up. "This is a day of rest."

"Not for the unrighteous," Stew Macon said, yanking the sheet down again. "Come on, Sam—there are forty-'leven reporters out there with umpty-two thousand questions to ask. They hear you got a fill-in last night and they're mad because you didn't tell them right away."

"I had my reasons," I said, sitting up. "The chief one being that I was dead tired. Earth's in one piece, isn't it? What more do they want?"

"They want a Monday paper story, what else? They said maybe you ought to have a whiff of that conscience gas yourself."

"All right." I got up and started to dress.

"Don't waste time shaving," Stew said. "They can stand you the way you are."

I shaved anyway, using the time to sort out what I was going to tell them.

They were there with their notebooks and sheafs of copy paper and lapel tape recorders and cameras, gathered impatiently in one of Ultra's big conference rooms. There was a magnificent close-up view of the moon through a transparent section of the hull, but no one was paying any attention to it.

My confreres, the British, French, Russian and other information officers or press secretaries, were seated behind a long table on a dais. An empty chair near the center of the table was flanked by Joy Linx and that Monolithian, Frij, who masqueraded as Addison Madison.

I took my seat and the UPI man jumped up and said, "Can we start now? Sam, tell us more about this conscience gas. How did it get to Domingo Sanchez? Was it dropped over his capital or piped into his office through the air conditioning, or what?"

That was an easy one. Frij had briefed me fully on that the night before.

"Simple," I said. "They rigged his microphone. You know the one he goes to every day to harangue the multitude and blast the big powers."

"Of course we know," the UPI said, "but *how?*"

"An American technician did it. Despite his anti-U.S. diatribes, Domingo Sanchez still needs American help locally. The technician sprayed the microphone with the gas, using a sort of pocket atomizer. Domingo breathed in the fumes his own moist breath activated."

"What does the gas do," a network correspondent asked; "affect the nerve centers of the brain?"

"Something like that. It makes the subject acutely aware of any suffering he is capable of causing. It has the psychological effect of making him actually feel the hurt he intends before he inflicts it. The more drastic the act he contemplates, the greater his pain. He can relieve the pain only by a clear-cut decision not to inflict the hurt."

"How long does this effect last?" a science writer asked. "Can't Domingo send the planes back up again when it wears off?"

I looked at Frij, but Joy had already shoved a piece of paper across to me. I read it quickly.

"No," I said. "The effect is permanent."

There was a stir in the room, and someone asked, "You mean Domingo Sanchez, erstwhile scourge of the Caribbean, is now and forever more on the side of the angles?"

I waited for the laughter to die down and said, "That's right. There shouldn't be any more trouble from El Spaniola—as long as the present regime lasts."

"Oh," the UPI man said, "then this gas was used only on Domingo Sanchez. It's not transferable? You know what I mean—contagious, like a cold?"

"It's not communicable in the way a disease is, but it doesn't necessarily have to be administered individually. One pellet no bigger than the end of my thumb, for example, would be enough to gas everybody in this room. I have a fact-sheet on the gas that I'll hand out to you after the press conference. I think it will answer most of the technical questions you may have. Its formula, of course, remains a Monolithian secret."

The Reuters man had a question for the British press officer: "Now that the Spaniola threat is ended, when does the super-summit meeting start and what's it all about? What's the agenda?"

"The conference is already in progress," the Briton said.

"How long will it last? What are they discussing?"

"They are discussing the future of mankind and it will go on as long as is necessary."

"Who represents Monolithia?" a French correspondent asked.

The French press officer shrugged and turned to Frij who, in his best Addison Madison manner, smiled and said, "That's a good question, old man. They haven't lifted the veil on that one."

"What are we going to call him in our stories? At least give us his title."

"I'll try to pry it out of them," Frij said. "Meanwhile, why not call him Mr. M.? That stands for Monolithia, I hasten to add. It isn't necessarily his initial."

That was about as far as anyone went. There were a few more questions, which drew vague or uninformative replies, and then the briefing ended with the promise that the press would be informed when the super-summit conference was over and that any communiqué would be expedited.

I hurried after the UPI man to ask about something that had been puzzling me. "Hey," I said, "where's the AP?"

"In his cabin, sick as a dog. His old intestinal trouble's acting up again. He never should have come on this junket."

"What about his story?" I asked. "Anybody going to file for him?"

"Don't worry. As soon as we get our own stories off, we're going to chip in and do one under his byline."

"That's damn nice of you."

"Nuts," the UPI said. "You've done the same thing in your time."

The way he put it made me realize how far out of things I was. I was beginning to feel like the tiresome old P.R. man who keeps telling people how he used to be a newspaper man himself.

The reporters had all gone off to file their stories and the only ones left in the conference room were Frij, Joy and the press officers. Frij and Joy were talking by themselves. I wandered over.

"I suppose you've got lots of this conscience gas," Joy was saying.

"Sufficient unto our needs," Frij said in his irritating way.

"Is there any here on Ultra?" I asked him. "I'd like to see what it looks like."

"Like many gases, it's invisible, as well as being odorless and tasteless. Joy, why don't you take our curious young man on a guided tour of Ultra? He's been so busy since he arrived that he hasn't had a chance to give it more than a once-over."

When we were out of earshot Joy said, "I guess you don't like Frij much, either."

"He's the first of them to rub me that way," I said. "Most of them are quite charming."

"It's my personal opinion they're all queer," Joy said.

"You mean homosexuals?"

"Either that or the Monolithian equivalent. Maybe I put it too strongly, but there's something wrong with them."

"Well, they're aliens, after all. You can't expect them to be just like us."

"No, but I've taken that into consideration. They don't have any women."

"Most explorers don't. Columbus didn't. The women come later, when the men have made things easier for them."

"Ha!" Joy said. "Go tell that to the Israeli women."

"You know what I mean."

We had made our way up the inner spiral ramp to the topmost part of the sphere.

"I guess I'm supposed to show you the view," Joy said.

"Behold the moon. And, yonder, the stars. We don't seem to be able to see Earth from here. I hope it's still intact... Who's that?"

It was a man kneeling close to the transparent outer edge of the corridor. We had startled him. He got to his feet, guiltily, then saw who we were.

"Oh, hello, Sam. Hello, Joy." It was Rod Harris of the AP. "Come here. Have a look at this."

"I thought you were sick," I said.

"I must be sick," Rod said. "I'm seeing double."

"Let me feel your head," Joy said. "I'll bet you have a fever."

"By all means feel my head. A pleasure. But that isn't what's the matter with me. Look out there. See those shiny things fastened to the hull at the ends of those long rods?"

"I see them," Joy said. "They're like silver Christmas tree ornaments. What are they?"

"I don't know what they're for," Rod said. "Maybe they're solar batteries or radar. Anyway they act just like mirrors. Look in that one. See? It lets you see right into one of the rooms. It's hard to tell at first, but I think I've got it figured out that the room's on the level just below us—what they call B Deck."

"I see it now. There must be a dozen or more people in there. Hey, they must be the VIPs! There's Gov, and the Russian and the Indian—"

"That's who they are, Joy. Can you make out what they're doing?"

"As far as I can see they're not doing a thing except lounging back in big chairs. They don't seem to be talking. I can't even tell if they've got their eyes open."

"They haven't," Rod said. "They're all asleep—or unconscious. Okay? Now look at that reflector—over there, to the left. No, higher. There. Now what do you see?"

"That's Gov! The President again!"

"Good. Now look in the next room. The man with the mustache—who's that?"

"The British Prime Minister?"

"Right," Rod said excitedly. "Now look into the room on the other side of Gov's. Here, shift over this way a little. There."

"That must be my room," I said. "Hey, there's somebody in it. Going through my suitcase. He won't find much. He looks vaguely familiar but I can't make out who he is."

"No wonder he looks familiar, Sam," Joy said. "That's you!"

"She's right, Sam," Rod said. "That's either you or your double. Do you have any idea what the hell's going on?"

It was me, all right—or my double. If you've ever seen yourself in a home movie, or on a TV monitor you know how it takes a second or so for you to recognize yourself on the screen—probably because you're so used to full-face reversed image you get in the bathroom mirror every morning. My double, apparently having found nothing in my things, took a last look around and let himself out into the corridor, where we lost sight of him.

"Well?" Rod said. "Want to chase him with me?"

"No," I said. "It wouldn't do any good. He's a Monolithian. So are all the other duplicates."

"Well," Rod said. "I see where you and I ought to have a good long talk. You know all this for a fact?"

I nodded. "Yes. All right, Rod. If I tell you what I know—and what I'm beginning to suspect—will you print it?" The fact that my duplicate was here in Ultra and not down in Bethesda where he would be capable of hurting Mae had something to do with my decision to spill to the AP.

"Every damn word, Sam," Rod Harris said.

Joy shrieked when the interior wall of the corridor slid back, revealing a Monolithian pointing a weapon of some sort at us.

The Monolithian smiled. "Miss Linx and gentlemen, I regret to inform you that censorship has just been imposed."

No matter how thin you slice it,
it's still baloney.
—Al Smith

CHAPTER TWENTY-ONE
(AUG. 11, MON.)

"RESISTANCE would have been futile, I suppose," Joy Linx said.

We were Monday-morning quarterbacking our capture, now nearly 24 hours old.

"Never argue with a man with a gun," Rod Harris said. "Old city-desk adage."

We were in a big room, much more luxurious then my previous Monolithian cell, and which we judged to be at Ultra's dead center. It had a wall-to-wall carpet, four couches, some straight chairs; a big bare desk and indirect lighting. There were two doors—the one we'd come in through and another to a well-equipped bathroom, which afforded our only privacy from each other. We'd slept in our clothes on the couches without blankets. It had been chilly.

We'd had no visitors except a Monolithian who brought us food but no enlightenment about our fate. He said not a word to us.

In the morning we took turns in the bathroom, Rod and I shaving and Joy fixing her face and untousling her hair.

"How about the next time the waiter comes in we jump him?" Joy asked.

"And how about him shooting us right in the head?" I said. "You notice he keeps his gun right under the tray."

"Better to be a live coward than a dead hero," Rod said. "Old copy-desk maxim."

"Never saw such levelheaded, clear-thinking captives," Joy said. "I admire your restraint."

"He who lives to run away may file his story another day," Rod said. "Old—"

"Don't tell me. Old front-office memo. Well, what's your story going to say, if you ever get to file it?"

"It's going to say Monolithians are no damn good. It's going to say they should go back where they came from, since they don't like it here. On Earth, I mean."

"It seems to be us they don't like," I said. "Let's write a story, Rod. It'll be something to do."

"Sure, why not? Even if it's published posthumously."

"That's what I like," Joy said. "Optimism. All right, you ace reporters, go ahead and write your story. You can even dictate it to me. I've got the old pad in the old handbag."

Joy took out her steno pad and poised a pencil over it.

Rod lay back on one of the couches. "Fair enough. How shall we start, Sam?"

"Dateline," I said. "Ultra, August whatever-it-is—eleven? That part's easy. Then what? AP? WW?"

"No," Rod said. "Special to the Free Press of the World. By Sam Kent and Rod Harris."

"As told to Joy Linx," I said.

"Sure, put that down," Rod said. "It's going to look like one of those six-man bylines in the *New York Post,* but what the hell."

"Thank you, gentlemen. Shall I read back what I've got so far?"

"Don't be flippant. Now let's see. A good lead is half the story. How about, 'Probably the most fantastic plot in Earth's history was being hatched today on the Monolithian super-satellite Ultra.'"

"Take out the 'probably,'" I said. "Earth never had an extraterrestrial plot before."

"Good desk man's deletion. That's giving it the whambo-zambo. Now, second sentence—new paragraph: 'A conspiracy involving substitution of Earth's leading statesmen by Mono-lithians impersonating them down to the last birthmark'—is that the way you see it, Sam?"

"Exactly," I said. "'...down to the last birthmark threatens to reduce the world to the status of a colony in an alien empire.'"

"Good," Rod said. "I see we're talking on the same channel. Now: 'The seemingly friendly Monolithians, who made such a well-publicized point of allying themselves, through the United Nations, with Earth's highest aspirations toward peace and brotherhood...'"

We must have worked on it for two hours. When Joy had taken it all down and we'd gone over it with the old editorial pencil, it read like this:

by Sam Kent and Rod Harris
as told to Joy Linx

ULTRA, Aug. 11 (Special to the Free Press of the World)— The most fantastic plot in Earth's history unfolded today in the Monolithian super-satellite Ultra.

A conspiracy involving substitution of Earth's leading statesmen by Monolithians impersonating them down to the last birthmark threatened to reduce the world to the status of a colony in an alien empire.

The seemingly friendly Monolithians who publicly allied themselves with Earth's highest aspirations toward peace and brotherhood have been unmasked as schemers and plotters bent on conquest—conquest by bloodless subversion if possible, but by force if necessary.

Events have made it clear that the ordinary people of Earth, their doubts stilled by the fact that their trusted leaders had agreed to a super-summit meeting, had no way of knowing the great pressures that had been brought to bear on their presidents and prime ministers.

The recent "peril"—that of the alleged threat to annihilate the world's major cities by Spaniolan O-bombs—has been revealed by authoritative sources as a gigantic hoax.

These sources, who include an official close to the President of the United States, are convinced that the threat never existed. They said it was an incident manufactured by the Monolithians with the willing cooperation of the Spaniolan dictator, General Domingo Sanchez, whose reward was to be the role of ruler of the Caribbean. He, too, is expected to find that he's been a dupe of the aliens, it was learned, and may not live to reap his reward.

The O-bombs he professed to have were nonexistent, these sources said. While it seems likely that the Monolithians do possess the "conscience gas" which reportedly ended the threat, there is extreme doubt that it was actually used on Domingo Sanchez—simply because he was a willing tool of the Monolithians and it wasn't necessary.

It is believed that knowledge of part of the plot was the factor that induced Earth's leaders to agree to the so-called super-summit meeting here. The Monolithians told them that the Spaniolan bombers—accompanied by refueling planes able to keep them aloft indefinitely—were already airborne and en route to the target cities. Disguised as commercial jet airliners and flying regular flight lanes, they avoided challenge by air defense forces.

Faced with the potential destruction of their cities, the world's leaders were forced to agree to the fantastic trip through space, in alien craft, to Ultra. "They were not naive, as many supposed," one high official said. "They were taking what they believed was the only step possible to save the lives of millions of innocent people."

Thus the Monolithians, who held out hope of preventing this unparalleled massacre, were able to entice Earth's top statesmen into the trap.

Once in Ultra, accompanied only by aides and a few military personnel armed feebly with hand guns, they were sitting ducks for the next twist of the alien plot.

This was the great substitution of incredibly well-trained Monolithians—transformed by alien medico-science into exact duplicates—for the presidents of the United States and France, the Prime Minister of Great Britain, the Premier of the Soviet Union, the Chancellor of Germany, and the others who went on the ill-fated journey.

From here, the future course of the plot is plain to see. The fake leaders, acclaimed by their people as the saviors of, humanity, will be able to do no wrong. Their declarations of faith in the motives of the Monolithians will go unchallenged.

The next step—the absolute domination of Earth by the Monolithians—will be a short and terrible one.

There was no typewriter in the room, so Joy had transcribed it into longhand.

We were reading the story over and wondering aloud how, if ever, we were going to file it when the door opened. Rod quickly dropped the pages behind the couch.

Our jailer shoved another prisoner into the room and shut the door again. It was Spookie Masters, comedian, bon vivant and world traveler, looking sheepish.

"Pardon the intrusion, folks," Spookie said.

"I didn't know you were aboard," Rod said. "For pete's sake, Spookie, what happened?"

"I stowed away," he said, his usual self-assurance returning. "Didn't want to be left out of this great development in the affairs of men."

"Stowed away?" Joy said admiringly. "How could you? I thought security was as tight as a drum." The hero worship the entertainer always managed to evoke in women was shining in Joy's eyes.

"I guess I oversimplified," Spookie said. "Actually I used pull. Bill Overton's an old friend of mine and I persuaded him to have Gov smuggle me aboard in the guise of a fifth assistant undersecretary. Just consider me one of the striped-pants set."

Overton was only the Secretary of the Treasury. Spookie Masters seemed to know everybody.

"Yeah," Rod told him, "but somewhere along the line you goofed."

"That I did, Roddy my boy. I dropped the jolly old brick. I got bored playing diplomat and started wandering around. Just strolling, and having a look into this comer and that, you know, when it began to dawn on me that everything wasn't strictly kosher."

"For instance?" I asked.

"Little things at first, Sam." I was pleased as a cub that he'd remembered my name. "Like when I wandered into a funny room where they were faking messages between Ultra and Earth."

"How do you mean?"

"Well, it was full of teletypes, like an Army message center I once had the misfortune to be assigned to. It seemed to be a Monolithian relay point. All the stories your colleagues filed passed through it—and they were all being edited or censored. And the incoming cables, or whatever you call them, were getting the same treatment. Lots of bright young men hard at work, doctoring the news of the world. Government messages, too. All Monolithians, I gather—but guess who their boss was, Sam."

"Who?"

"You. I gave you the big hello and you gave me the big vacant stare, and so I got out of there. I'm not an egomaniac, exactly, but I did think it a bit strange that you didn't remember ol' Spookie Masters."

"That wasn't me," I said. "I saw him, too."

"I didn't know then there were two of you. But after I snooped some more and saw two Gov Allisons and two French presidents and two of all the rest, it percolated fast that there was a big deficiency in the up-and-up department. By that time the boys in the wool cloaks were hot on my tail and I ended up here with you other charming spies. I presume that's what you're in for too."

"Where did you see these two sets of summiteers?" Rod asked. "I gather it wasn't long ago."

"Just a few minutes ago," Spookie said. "It was at the big porthole thing—you know, where we transferred from the spaceship. Only they were going out—one set into one spaceship and the other into a second. It's just a hunch, of course, but I sort of got the impression that the wrong presidents were going back to Earth."

He who is wrapped in purple robes,
With planets in His care,
Had pity on the least of things
Asleep upon a chair.
—William Butler Yeats

CHAPTER TWENTY-TWO
(AUG. 12, TUES.)

MAYBE IT WAS our high-class company, or maybe it was just that the Monolithians figured everything was going swimmingly for them. Whatever the reason, they treated us royally after Spookie Masters joined our little captive society.

The cuisine improved. Our jailers brought in cigarettes and cigars and fairly recent copies of *Harper's* and *The New Yorker*. They rolled back a wall so Joy Linx could have a private bedroom and handed out blankets all around. They even brought in typewriters and stacks of copy paper. It was all quite cozy, except that we were still prisoners and that none of our captors ever spoke to us.

Spookie came out of the bathroom, wiping leftover lather off his face, and said, "What are they doing? I don't want to settle down here. We've got to find a way to bust out of this joint."

"Now," Rod said, "if that isn't an ace-high, triple-plated, razzle-dazzle idea, I've never heard one." He was having a second cup of our breakfast coffee. "And just how do you think we should carry out your splendid plan, Mr. Masters?"

"Cut it out, Rod," Spookie said. "I know I talk big. But have we explored all the possibilities? I suppose you've gone over this room with a fine-tooth comb, but how about Joy's? Maybe there's some way out from there."

"Miss Linx is still enjoying her beauty sleep," Rod said. "But it's a thought. Let's rout her out."

But the door opened and Joy said, "I heard that, you fiends. First respectable night's sleep I had, too, since I was thrown in among you great big leering men."

"Don't lump me in with these raffish reporters, ma'am," Spookie said. "I'm the soul of honor."

"I treat that remark with the doubt it deserves," Joy said. "But all this gay banter aside, men, I've been tinkering with a thought. Were you watching when they opened up the wall to make my room? Well, I was. There was a certain way our woolly friend touched the wall. Maybe if we felt around on the other side in here..."

We gave the wall a thorough going-over, fingering it, rapping on it and occasionally kicking it in frustration. Just as we were about to give up, it rolled back, revealing another room, bare except for some crates. There was a door to the corridor and Spookie went to it quickly. It opened easily and he peered out through a crack.

"Nobody out there," he said. "Let's go!"

I had opened the only one of the crates whose lid wasn't fastened down. It was filled nearly to the top with flat, black boxes about the size of a paperback book. I had no idea what they were but slipped several into my jacket pockets before following the others into the corridor.

It was still empty after we'd slunk quite a distance from our plush prison. We went down the spiral ramp, trying to head back to the press room, on the theory that we'd be safer among our own kind—though it was obvious now that every Earthman aboard was at the mercy of the Monolithians. Rod had our story and his chief interest at the moment was finding a way to file it to Earth uncensored.

Spookie went first, then Rod, followed by Joy. I brought up the rear.

I hadn't tied my shoes and they were flopping against the bare floor, making a racket. I stopped to tie them and the others disappeared around the bend.

Before I could catch up with them a Monolithian had caught me.

For a fraction of a second I didn't recognize him. He'd come up quietly behind me and just stood there until I noticed him.

"Hello, Sam," he said. "No, don't get up."

I remained on one knee and automatically finished the knot I was making as I looked up.

The fraction of a second over, I saw who it was. Me.

I tried to think of something to do or say, but all I could do was stare in fascination. He looked just a trifle wrong, but again I realized almost immediately that this was only because I was seeing not the mirror image I was used to, but an exact, unreversed duplicate.

He was looking at me with an almost hypnotic stare. My mind began to falter, like a car engine with bad cylinders.

"Up now, but slowly," my Monolithian duplicate said. He didn't seem to be armed. He was dressed exactly as I was, in jacket and slacks.

I got to my feet, unable to look away from his eyes.

"You are powerless to do anything except what I tell you," he said. It was true. I was only half thinking now, my attention concentrated on this superbly confident other self of mine. Somewhere among the missing cylinders, however, was my recollection that this was the creature who had taken my place in bed with Mae. My head hurt at the thought, coupled with his proximity. I longed to take him by the neck and throttle him until he was dead, dead, dead. But I was powerless to move except as he directed.

Then Joy came back around the bend behind him. I threw myself against him and he fell off balance. She had only a few seconds to take in the situation. She swung up her handbag and gave him a good clout on the head. He crumpled to the floor. She hit him again, on the downswing, and the sharp metal corner of her bag banged into his skull. He was out.

"Thanks, Joy. You're a lifesaver."

"Maybe," she said. "If we don't get out of here we'll both be more like wads of second-hand chewing gum. What are you *doing?*"

I'd pulled my unconscious image to a sitting position against the wall of the corridor and was going through his pockets.

"Little identity switch," I told her.

He had nothing at all in his inside breast pocket, but there was a clip-on pencil and a small notebook in his shirt pocket. I exchanged them for the little notebook and clip-on pencil I keep in the same place. I exchanged wallets, too, not without a pang for the eighty-odd dollars in expense money that was in mine. I put off examining his. For good measure I switched the handkerchiefs we both carried in our right hip pockets and the few coins in the change pockets of our jackets.

"Looks like a fair exchange," Joy said. "Now what? Can't we hurry up?"

"Where are the others?"

"I don't know. I came back when I missed you."

I found a door that opened and pulled my duplicate into the room. It was an empty cabin, obviously unused. I propped him against a chair and Joy said, "Shall I give him another whack?"

"No, let's just leave him. We don't want to kill the guy. He looks as if he'll be out for quite a while."

We decided to head for the landing stage. On the way I asked Joy about something that had been puzzling me: "Just how did you know which one of us to hit?"

She thought for a moment. "Intuition, I guess. You were the one who was attacking—using physical violence—so you couldn't have been the Monolithian. He would have been armed with one of his super weapons. I didn't really think about it." She looked at me and said, apparently only half jokingly, "You *are* you, aren't you?"

My head was beginning to throb again. "I hope so."

We reached the big open area near the landing stage.

"This is where we have to look very matter-of-fact," I told Joy. "I have a small hunch. Just play it by ear."

There were only a few people near the transparent airlock. All but one of them wore the Monolithian woolen cloaks. I didn't recognize the man dressed in Earth clothing. He certainly wasn't one of the reporters.

Joy and I tried to stroll nonchalantly toward the airlock. I had only the vaguest of plans for finding out as subtly as possible when the next flight—if any—left for Earth.

One of the cloaked men came toward us. He smiled. "Mr. Kent?"

"That's right."

"Your ID card, please."

I handed him the wallet I'd appropriated. He unfolded it and looked for a long few seconds at the White House card under the cellophane window. Then he handed the wallet back.

"Yes, sir," he said. "Your pilot is ready, as arranged. Will the lady be accompanying you?"

"Yes," I said. "My secretary, Miss Linx." The throb in my head was worse. I supposed it was the tension.

"Okay, Sam." He winked. He turned and gave an order. The inner pane of the airlock rose swiftly and a tiny craft, no more than three times the size of my Volkswagen, rolled out from the side. Joy and I walked toward it. So did the one man in Earth clothing. Without a glance at us, he went into the pilot's compartment forward.

Joy and I had reached the steps leading to the passenger space aft when the Monolithian in the cloak said, "One last thing, Mr. Kent. The last formality."

Throb-throb, went my head. Joy looked at me questioningly and put her hand inside my elbow. I squeezed it to my body.

"All right," I said as if annoyed. "Let's get it over with." There was just the slightest trace of suspicion in his eyes as he said, "What word from you shall I send to our colleagues?"

The throbbing in my skull grew more intense. "Duty," I said, not knowing why. But I said it firmly.

The Monolithian nodded. "And—?"

"Duty and dedication," I said without hesitation. My head felt as if Buddy Rich and Zutty Singleton and Gene Krupa were all pounding away inside. I was genuinely annoyed now. "Let's go," I said sharply. "There's no time to lose."

"You're right," the Monolithian said. Joy and I got in and he went up to the pilot, his suspicions apparently at rest, and told him, "Take Mr. Kent and Miss Linx to Earth."

The only way to get rid of a
temptation is to yield to it.
—Oscar Wilde

CHAPTER TWENTY-THREE
(AUG. 13, WED.)

THE PILOT said virtually nothing to us on the long trip, except that during the final orbital glide he asked me where I wanted to get out. I said I'd prefer it to be as close as possible to downtown Washington. His cockpit was completely isolated from the passenger compartment and we communicated by intercom. I was sure he could hear everything Joy and I said, so we talked only inconsequentials and spent quite a bit of the time dozing in our comfortable lounge chairs.

The pilot took me at my word and landed on the mall near the Washington Monument. It was just getting dark.

He said, "Duty," and I replied, "Duty and dedication." He took off again without another word.

Joy and I watched his silent climb into the sky. So did a few pedestrians and the group of people waiting to go up to the Monument. A policeman started toward us, not running but with a purposeful walk, so I hailed a cab and we got away from there.

"Where to?" the driver asked.

"White House," I said, to give him some place to head for. He drove off. The cop decided not to chase us.

Joy said, "We can't go to the White House. We'd be walking right into their jaws."

"I know," I said. "But if they were after us we'd never have got this far. Our dutiful pilot would have seen to that."

"They must have found the fake Sam Kent by now," Joy, said. "They can't still think you're him. Something's fishy."

"You're right, of course. We'd better catch up on what's been going on."

162

"We'll go to my place," Joy said. She gave the driver a South-East address and said to me, "We can listen to the newscasts and pick up the papers on the way."

Joy lived in a top-floor apartment in a new building from which you could see the dome of the Capitol.

"There's the radio and TV and there's something in the cabinet over the sink in the kitchen if you want to make a drink," she said. "Make yourself at home. I'm going to take a shower and get into some different clothes. I've been in this outfit so long it feels like a uniform."

I'd bought the *Post,* the *Star,* the *News,* the *Baltimore Sun* and the *New York Times.* I dropped them and myself on the couch and turned on the radio. She'd had it tuned to WGMS and for a while I got nothing but good music. I looked over the front pages to muted sounds of Mozart and the bathroom shower.

The morning papers, the *Post* and *Times,* had similar headlines, something to the effect that a blueprint for interplanetary peace had been charted at the Ultra summit conference.

The afternoon papers headlined the return to Earth of the summiteers. The tabloid *News* said all over its front page:

GOV BACK FROM SPACE;
HAILS SUMMIT TALK AS
'TRIUMPH FOR MANKIND'

The conservative *Star* gave it an eight-column banner:

WORLD LEADERS RETURN FROM ULTRA;
CONFERENCE WITH MONOLITHIANS SEEN
INSURING GENERATIONS OF PEACE

I looked in vain for the story Rod Harris and I had written, or for anything like it. There was no hint anywhere that the threat of El Spaniola had been a hoax and certainly no indication that the President and his fellow chiefs of state were any different than before they'd left for Ultra.

Nor was there any word about Gov's press secretary being missing. In fact there were several quotes from good old Samuel L. C. Kent, saying in substance that there was nothing that could be added to what was in the official statements and giving a few homey details about how the President had enjoyed his first trip into space.

"He had a fine time," I was quoted as saying at Dulles International Airport, where the spaceships had landed on their return from Ultra, "and he looks forward to making another trip—perhaps even to Monolithia itself after he leaves the White House."

What this meant, of course, was that my double had got loose in time to rejoin the other duplicated Earthpeople before they got back to Washington. It also meant that the Monolithians had known who I was during my flight back with Joy and that they had a good reason for not stopping us. I wondered what that reason was.

The throbbing in my head began again.

Joy came out of the bathroom wearing an extremely attractive wrapper, belted rather insecurely at the waist. She'd washed her hair and had combed it straight back in a ponytail. She wore no makeup except lipstick and had, left off her glasses. She was barefoot and desirable. I wanted to kiss her.

"Well," she said, "that's a lot better. Nothing like getting rid of the grime of two planets. What, no drink, Mr. Sam? You *are* a dedicated one."

"Do something for me, Joy. Call my home and ask for me. If I'm not there make some excuse and hang up."

"All right." She went to the phone. "And if you are there?"

"Hang up anyway."

She dialed the Bethesda number. It answered almost immediately.

"Hello," I heard her say; "is Jim there...? James Fairchild... Oh, isn't this Empire 3-6573...? I'm sorry; I must have the wrong number." She put the phone down and said to me, "It was you."

Throb-throb. My head again. It wasn't a pain but an insistent hammering in the center of my skull.

"That means Mae's with…him," I said. "And she thinks it's me again."

"Poor Sam. I'm going to make you a good stiff Scotch. You need it."

"I need something." Maybe cold water would help. "I think I'll take a shower while you fix the drinks. It's awfully hot."

"Help yourself. The folded towel is the dry one."

I took off my jacket and dropped it on the couch. In the bathroom I noticed that Joy squeezed her toothpaste tube from the middle, just like Mae. She had various wispy nylon things drying on racks and used a perfume called *Suivez-moi*, I picked up the bottle and sniffed it. Throb-throb.

I turned on the shower full cold, undressed and stood under it. The pounding in my head eased. Shivering, I turned the handle toward hot and soaped.

When I emerged, Joy had put my jacket away and two tall drinks stood on the coffee table in front of the couch.

"Feel better?" she asked.

"Much." I sat down beside her and took a big swallow. She handed me a lit cigarette. It had lipstick traces on the filter end. Throb-throb.

"I prefer my lipstick firsthand," I said. I put the cigarette down and pulled her toward me. Her eyes looked into mine, then closed. I kissed her. The scent of *Suivez-moi* and the softness of her lips and body made the room tilt.

Her nails dug through my shirt into my back. Her lips went to my ear and she whispered, "Oh, Sam. I've wanted this for so long!"

Throb-throb. I was torn between two desires. This enchanting woman, whispering in my ear, her single garment— for that's all she wore—slipping off her shoulders, was a temptation that Sam Kent, Earthman, could not have resisted.

But the throbbing inside my skull reminded me that I was more than that. I was pseudo-Sam, the Monolithian man, bent on a greater mission. Duty and dedication were mine. I was no mere single entity. I was one of a group-one of many, all devoted to the same ideal. The distractions of Earth were nothing to me and easy to deny. I pushed Joy away from me. The throbs had become stabbing pains.

"A typewriter," I said flatly. "I require a typewriter." Joy sat up, pulling her wrapper around her. Her eyes, which a moment ago were melting, had grown cold.

"You want *what?*" she said icily.

"You heard me, Earthwoman," I said. "A typewriter. At once!"

Joy stood up. She gave me a look of hatred and went to her bedroom, slamming the door behind her.

I found Joy's portable in its case on the bottom shelf of the bookcase. I set it up on the coffee table, rolled a sheet into it and thought for a moment.

Then, spurred by pain, I typed:

"Now here on Earth do I declare myself, racked and driven by motives outside my understanding, to be not what I seem, nor yet entirely what I am. Blessed is he who knows himself wholly—"

I stopped typing. I wasn't saying it. I opened the window wide and shouted toward the Capitol:

"Hear this! The hour approaches! Mend your ways lest the evil consequences overtake you! Hear me, Earthlings! You are all a part of the greater scheme and each must take the responsibility. Hark, before it is too late!"

"Shut up, you drunk," said a voice from below.

I slammed the window and picked up the phone. "Give me Western Union. I want to send a telegram… Take this down and send it to the FBI and the CIA: This is bigger than your spies and your communist agents. Let me put you wise to an interstellar conspiracy. Drop everything else and arrest the President of the United States… Who? The supervisor? Get off the line, I'm dictating a vital telegram… I'll tell you who I am when I get to the signature… Well, nuts to you, Madam."

I hung up and ran into the kitchen. I turned on the cold water and stuck my head under the faucet. It eased the pain. I picked up the bottle of Scotch and swallowed three times, then ran gasping back to the telephone.

I dialed the *Washington Post's* number and asked for the city desk.

"Hello? Stop the presses! Tear out the front page! I've got a scoop for you. SCOOP. Take this down:

"I, Joe Spaceman, have defected from the Monolithians.

You can quote me on that. You got that so far…? What the hell do you mean, put it in a letter? You think I'm crazy…? Listen, you imbecile, if you don't know an exclusive when you hear it, you'd better go back to journalism school."

I hung up on him, the jerk, and went back to the typewriter.

"Dear Drew Pearson: Maybe you can wake up the world. It's sleeping on the brink. The vastest most incredible conspiracy in history is being perpetrated under the noses of the decent folk…"

There was a knock at the hall door. As I turned to tell whoever it was to go away, Joy flew out of her bedroom and opened it.

Spookie Masters came in, patted Joy on the shoulder and strode over to me. I got up.

"You can tell them, Spookie!" I said. "Go on television and tell them all. There's no time to lose. Tell them how—" Spookie pulled back his arm and I saw his fist coming at my chin.

O Cuckoo! shall I call thee bird,
Or but a wandering voice?
—Wordsworth

CHAPTER TWENTY-FOUR
(AUG. 14, THURS.)

4:45 A.M. My head was no longer throbbing when I came to, but my jaw ached and my mouth tasted of old blood.

I was lying on the couch, my arms tied behind me and my feet fastened together at the ankles with my own belt.

I could hear Spookie and Joy talking in the tiny kitchen. It was dark outside, with just a tinge of dawn in the sky.

I wasn't gagged, so I said, "Hey."

"Aha," Spookie said, looking around the doorway. "Our sleeper awakes. Who do you think you are now, Sam? Our old pal Kent or the King of the Outer Planets?"

"Damn you," I said. "Untie me."

"Maybe later. You're too much for us Earthlings to take chances with. You were really way out, little chum."

"I'm sorry," I said, beginning to remember.

"You'd better be," Joy said from around the corner. "You were absolutely outrageous. I'm making coffee. Want some?"

"Yes, please. How did Spookie get here? I thought he was still on Ultra."

"They've got a very efficient shuttle service," Spookie said. "They decided it'd be better to ship me back than to get themselves bad publicity by keeping me prisoner."

"Tell Sam how you threatened them," Joy said.

"With the undying wrath of the Spookie Masters Fan Club," Spookie said. "Three and a half million anti-Monolithians was more than they were willing to risk—especially teen-agers, who are inclined to be extreme."

"What an ego," I said. "Did Rod Harris come back with you?"

"He did. I left him at the AP, busting to file a story."

"How come they let him go?"

"My influence, I think," Spookie said. "You're sure full of questions for a reporter without a notebook."

"How did you get here? You didn't answer that one."

"I was anxious about Joy, naturally. I called her up and she told me she had a madman in her living room. Maidens in distress are my specialty."

"You did not call up," I said. "The phone never rang."

Joy answered that: "I happen to have another phone in my bedroom, with a private number. A good thing, too, the way you were carrying on. And if you want to know where Spookie got the number," she added defiantly, "I gave it to him. Any objections, *Mister* Kent?"

"No," I mumbled, considerably deflated. "I'm sorry, Joy—about lots of things."

"Forget it," she said. "How about some scrambled eggs?"

"You'll have to feed me."

Spookie said, "No. I think we'll risk untying your arms and see whose side you're on."

5:30 A.M. We had eaten—I politely, free-armed, with no trouble to my captors—and the sun was peeping through the morning haze when WGMS interrupted its music with a news bulletin.

"More coffee?" Joy said.

"Shh," I said, and the radio said:

"Bulletin from our newsroom. President Allison has just issued the following statement. Oh—one moment, please. Is this on the lev—"

The announcer hadn't hit the cough button quite soon enough. He was back after a moment of dead air, saying:

"We have now verified that this statement is actually from the President. According to all three American wire services, he called them personally before dawn. Here is President Allison's statement, exactly as he dictated it:

"'My dear fellow citizens. During the next few days you may hear a number of rumors which I wish to nip in the bud right now.

"'I hasten to assure you now, before these vicious lies spread, that they are fabrications designed to split your loyalties.

"'You will hear it said that I have been kidnapped and that an impersonator has taken my place in the White House. You will be asked to believe that all Earth's leaders have been abducted and that Monolithian duplicates have been substituted for them.

"'Let me repeat that this will be pernicious propaganda, spread by your enemies and mine, designed to undermine confidence in the great interstellar alliance for peace we have lately forged on Ultra.

"'Later today I will record, on tape and film, a similar message to you, my fellow citizens, to banish any lingering doubts you may have. I have asked our great radio and television networks to broadcast my message hourly throughout the day, so that you will both see and hear me give the lie to this outrageous plot to delude you and undermine your faith in your government and your President, who remains sincerely and genuinely yours—Gouverneur "Gov" Allison.'"

6:47 A.M. Telephone. The one in the living room. Joy, yawning, answered it.

"Yes, this is Joy Linx... Well, yes, sir—he does happen to be here..."

She said to me, "It's for you, Sam. I—I think it's the President."

"Or the man who sounds like him," Spookie said.

I took the phone. "Sam Kent speaking." I listened, rubbing one tingling leg against the other. I nodded. I said, "Yes, sir" several times. I hung up.

"I've got to go to the White House," I said to Joy and Spookie. To Joy I said, "Sorry about—"

"Never mind. You go on."

To Spookie I said, "Any objections, muscles?"

170

"Go on," he said.   "If you think you know what you're doing. But if you want my advice—"

"I don't."   I got my jacket and went out. Joy came to the door.

"Will you be all right—with him?" I asked.

She said, "Sure. Don't worry. I'm not worried about them." It wasn't till I was down in the street, looking for a cab, that I realized she'd said "them," not "him."

I didn't take the first cab that came along, nor the second. And when I hailed the third I said nothing about the White House. I told the driver to take me to a bus that would get me to Baltimore.

9 A.M.   Railroad station, Baltimore. Television. Image of Gov: "My dear fellow citizens…"

1 P.M. Pennsylvania Station, New York. Loudspeaker: "My dear fellow citizens…"

1:15 P.M.   IRT 7th Avenue Subway. Newspaper headlines. *Post:*   "GOV TELLS NATION: I'M ME; BEWARE RUMORS."

World-Telegram: "PRESIDENT SPIKES KIDNAP FEARS; HITS ENEMY LIES."

Journal-American: "WHO'S IN WHITE HOUSE? 'GOV' SAYS HE IS."

2:20 P.M. I got off the subway in Brooklyn, bypassed the St. George as being too well known, and registered at the Towers down the street as Edward Lang.

3:40 P.M. Hotel switchboard operator: "I'm sorry, sir, that number still doesn't answer. Shall I keep trying?"

"No, thanks. Get me room service, will you?"

4:45 P.M. Having eaten and sent my clothes to be pressed, I arranged to buy a white shirt and rent an electric shaver. I left a call for midnight and went to bed. The last voice I heard on the five o'clock news on WNBC was that of the man in the White House, whoever he was, saying, "...the great interstellar alliance for peace we have lately forged on Ultra..."

And if the blind lead the blind,
both shall fall into the ditch.
—Matthew, XV, 14

CHAPTER TWENTY-FIVE
(AUG. 15. FRI.)

THE PHONE RANG. It was the desk clerk saying it was 12:15 A.M.

I thanked him and asked him to get me the number I'd been unable to reach the previous afternoon. There was a reluctant answer on the eleventh ring.

"Hello?" a male voice said. To my surprise it was one I recognized.

"Is this Mr. Avery?"

"It should be," the voice said cautiously. "Who is this?"

"Sam Kent," I said.

"I thought so. Have you been trying to reach me? I've been out."

"I know, but now I'd like to see you. When can we meet?"

"Not now. It's after midnight."

"I know; but it's important."

"I suppose it is. Where are you?"

"Brooklyn," I said. "But not very deep. I can make it in half an hour."

"All right. But be careful."

"Of course."

My clean clothes were ready by then and I dressed. I made sure I had all the flat black boxes I'd swiped from Ultra.

When I was halfway to the subway I realized I was being followed. At the same instant my head began to throb, for the first time since I'd gone berserk in Joy's apartment. That seemed to mean my shadow was a Monolithian. I continued on toward the subway, walking a little faster. There were half a dozen people on the street behind me and I couldn't be sure which one of them was after me.

I bought some tokens at the change booth and asked the attendant a series of complicated questions about how to get to a fictitious address in Queens. Two men came down the stairs a few seconds apart and went onto the subway platform. Neither one looked at me, nor did I recognize either of them.

I prolonged my conversation at the change booth until a Manhattan-bound train came in. Both men boarded it. But the throb in my head continued. It was annoying but not painful.

I thanked the attendant and went through the turnstile. There was a long wait for the next train. Just as I'd gone in and sat down, a man came running through the turnstile and got into my nearly empty car a second before the doors closed.

He took a seat opposite and looked at me with a little smile. It could have been no more than the smile one stranger gives another at his small success in triumphing over a machine, but when the throbbing in my head intensified I knew it was more than that. This was my Monolithian shadow.

He was neatly dressed in a brown gabardine suit. He was sixtyish, hatless and wore gold-rimmed eyeglasses. He had a big, retired-English-officer type of mustache and looked vaguely familiar.

The train went through the East River tunnel and at the Wall Street station I got up as if to get out. My friend in gabardine stood up casually and strolled to the same door. I had thought of waiting till just before the doors closed, then stepping out, but he would have been right behind me. I walked down the car and picked up a *Daily News* someone had discarded.

My friend meanwhile pretended to study the subway map near the door, then sat down again, not quite opposite me.

The tabloid's headline reflected a non-Monolithian development in an international romance. PRINCE'S DREAM GIRL SHUNS YACHT TRYST, it said, making it clear that the *Daily News* was getting bored with interstellar intrigue. I looked in vain for the Rod Harris-Sam Kent expose.

I got out at Times Square, waiting till the last second. But my shadow was too quick to be fooled. He was right at my heels as the doors shut, then dropped back a few paces.

I went up the stairs and into a phone booth. I dialed the number of the man who called himself Mr. Avery while my shadow stood a dozen feet away, buying himself a cup of soda from an automatic vending machine and drinking it slowly.

"Hello?" Avery said.

"I'm at Times Square but I'm being followed," I said.

Instead of telling me to go back to my hotel, as I expected him to, Avery said, "Good!"

"That's good?"

"Perfect," Avery said. "You come right on up—and be sure not to lose him. We want him. How's your head?"

"Throbbing," I said. "What makes you ask?"

"Never mind. Just bring your friend. One thing—there's a little delicatessen on the corner just before you get to the apartment-house entrance. Pick up half a dozen cans of frozen orange juice on your way, will you?"

"Sure. Will it be open?"

"It's open till 3. Six cans. Don't forget."

"Okay."

I went back down to the subway platform. My gabardine friend followed me. I took an uptown local and got off at 91st Street, at not quite the last second. My shadow made it safely to the platform.

At the corner of Columbus Avenue I went into the delicatessen. The man behind the counter was a big Negro. He looked familiar, somehow. There were no other customers.

"Any frozen orange juice?" I asked.

My shadow came in and put coins into the cigarette machine.

"Yes, sir," the Negro said. "How many?"

"Six."

The Negro came out from behind the counter. He took six cans out of the freezer chest and put them in a heavy ice-cream bag. To the Monolithian he said, "Pardon me." Then he hit

175

him over the head with the six cans of frozen orange juice. My shadow crumpled to the floor.

The Negro pulled the shade down over the door and locked it. He put out most of the lights.

"I guess we can close up now, Mr. Kent," he said. "We'll go the back way, through the building."

My head had stopped throbbing.

I recognized the Negro as we went up in the freight elevator with the unconscious Monolithian.

"You're Timmie Johnson, aren't you?"

"That's right, Mr. Kent."

Timmie was Gov's valet and probably much more than that, I now realized.

The elevator doors opened at the top of the apartment house and Gov Allison stood there waiting. Half a dozen men were with him.

"Well done, Timmie," the President of the United States said. "You, too, Sam."

This is no time to get out the crying towel or to throw in the sponge.

—Richard M. Nixon

CHAPTER TWENTY-SIX
(AUG. 16, SAT.)

WE'D BEEN HEARING about it all day. The papers delivered to the top floor of the apartment house—the midtown-Manhattan hideout of Gov Allison, alias Mr. Avery, and his small band of anti-Monolithian guerrillas—were full of ads:

"Giant Rally at Madison Square Garden Tomorrow Night! Come One, Come All! Admission Free! Entertainment! Music! Souvenirs! Master of Ceremonies: Spookie Masters, Star of Stage, Screen and Television! Sponsored by the Monolithian-American Friendship Society."

There were spot announcements on radio and television, saying those who couldn't go to the rally would be able to watch it on the All-Network Telecast.

"Listen, Gov," I said. It was the first chance I'd had to ask him. "How did you get back to Earth? The last I heard, you and the other VIP's were being sent off to space somewhere while your Monolithian duplicates came back down."

Gov was drinking a screwdriver—possibly made from one of the six cans Timmie had used to knock out the Monolithian in the delicatessen.

"That's easy," Gov said. "I never went to Ultra."

"But I *saw* you go. So did everybody else."

"No," Gov said. "You saw my stand-in. I told you some time ago, Sam, when we first got into this Alien rat race, that I was a tired old President. Only a few people know that for the last eighteen months I haven't attended a single cornerstone laying or warship launching or one of those rose garden jobs with the Lion's Club or the Boy Scouts. My double—a retired actor you've probably never heard of—officiated at them all. And he's the one, poor fellow, who's out there in space now. I hope he's all right. Fix me another one of these, will you, Sam?"

"Listen, Josh," I said to Joshua Holcomb, the original and now undercover White House Press Secretary whose job I had publicly taken, "if Gov is so all-fired lazy and ineffectual, what's he doing leading the underground? Frankly, I'm confused."

"Don't worry about a thing, Sam," Josh said. "You've done a great job, in your own way. I wouldn't be surprised if you got the Medal of Merit out of this, one day."

That's all I got out of *him*.

"Listen, Timmie," I said to the sometime White House valet, Timmie Johnson, "where'd they hide that Monolithian you conked with the orange juice? Who is he? And just what the hell is going on, anyway?"

"Mr. Kent," he said, "I think you'd just better wait and see. Oh—Mr. Gov asked me to ask you: have you got those boxes you took from Ultra? The CW boys want to have a look at them."

They'd been in my pocket ever since I broke out of the plush cell I'd shared with Rod and Joy. I handed them over gladly. Timmie went out.

They were all as busy as birds at nest-building time. I was the only one in the place who had nothing to do. That gave me time to think, which I didn't want. My thoughts always ended with Mae, my wife, and the impossibility of my returning to her while my Monolithian duplicate was with her. I couldn't risk confronting Mae, especially now, in her pregnancy, with the shock of realizing there were two Sam Kents and that she had been swapped between us in a sort of game of musical beds.

I couldn't think about this very hard, either, without getting fairly unstable and wanting to put my fist through something.

My only comfort was Joy Linx's stray thought that the Monolithians might be homosexuals.

I had various other thoughts during the time nobody was talking to me and I was feeling useless.

The thoughts, mostly unanswered questions, were roughly as follows:

How big was Gov's organization? Did it consist of anyone besides the handful of men in this apartment? What did it hope to accomplish?

What caused the throbbing in my head? It seemed to occur only when I was close to a Monolithian—my duplicate on Ultra and the man who'd shadowed me here, for example. Were any of the other duplicated Earthmen similarly affected? Gov, for instance? I'd have to ask him.

And what did it signify—a form of Monolithian control?

Point to remember: the throbbing stopped when the Monolithian lost consciousness.

Why was Spookie Masters emceeing the big Sunday night rally? I'd got the impression that he'd lost his enchantment with the aliens after his experience as their captive on Ultra. But it was possible that the rally had been arranged before that incident, and there was no time to change the plans for it. It would be interesting to see what Spookie's attitude would be when he got up in front of the mike at the Garden.

I wondered if Joy would be there. I also wondered, with a twinge of what I tried to assure myself was not jealousy, whether Spookie was still in her apartment in Washington and whether she'd succumbed by now to his well-known charm.

Gov Allison wandered in, looking unhappy.

I started to get up, but he waved me back on the couch. He dropped himself at the other end of it and put his head back, rubbing his forehead.

"My head hurts," he said. "Must be the late hours. Not used to them. What time is it, anyway?"

It was about 2 P.M., I told him. "How does it hurt, Mr. President? I mean, is it a sharp pain, or—"

"It's a dull throb," he said. "Maybe a screwdriver would help. Would you mind looking in that cabinet over there, Sam, and seeing if there are any fixings?"

"Sure." I made myself one, too, then told him about my own headaches and my theory that they were caused by the proximity of Monolithians. It was interesting that Gov was experiencing the throbbing now and I was not.

"Where's the Monolithian we captured?" I asked. "I'll bet he's the one behind your headache."

"They've been working over him all day," Gov said. "In a thoroughly humane way, of course," he added quickly. "With drugs and things. We can't afford to cast the first stone in this situation."

"Have you found out why he was tailing me?"

"They haven't told me what they've found out, if anything. I think they want to get it all sorted out and translated into layman's terms first. Then we'll do something about it, when they've worked out a few ideas. I'm a decider, you know, not a planner."

Josh Holcomb walked in, looking excited.

"Gov," he said. "I think it's time you came in."

They had the Monolithian strapped to a doctor's examining table. He was naked.

"My God," Gov said. "He's a woman! Or is he?"

It was easy to see why Gov was confused. The Monolithian had none of the male paraphernalia at his loins. But he had no breasts, either, though otherwise he seemed to be a fully developed adult.

"The subject appears to have no reproductive apparatus whatever," a man in a uniform said. I learned later that he was Brigadier General Horton Shales, the assistant White House physician.

The subject, as General Shales called him, was lying with his legs together, so this wasn't something you could tell at a glance.

He had more than the usual amount of pubic hair, but his chest was as hairless as Hollywood's Tarzans'. He had opened his eyes when we came in, then closed them again. His face was absolutely expressionless.

"Hmm," Gov said after a moment of thought. "How does he go to the bathroom?"

"It doesn't," Shales said. "There's no anal orifice either. In fact—" he paused, either for dramatic effect or to choose his words and avoid being technical "—the subject is not a human being. It is an imitation of one—an android."

Gov thought that over. Then he said:

"I see he has a good-sized mustache. But it doesn't look as if he shaves."

"A good observation," Shales said. "We restored its disguise temporarily—the glasses, false mustache and wig. We'll remove them again now… There."

"My God," Gov said again. "It's me!" It was, too; the android was his exact duplicate—at least from the neck up.

"How many of them *are* there?" Gov asked.

I could imagine him enumerating them in his mind: his stand-in out in space, his double in the White House, himself, and now this on the examining table.

The latest of the duplicates opened its eyes then and looked at Gov, who grabbed his forehead and moaned. I felt a little throb myself, as if I were getting the overflow.

"Do something, Doc," I said to General Shales. "It's got some kind of hold on Gov's mind."

Shales quickly picked up a hypodermic and jabbed it into the android's arm. Its eyes closed after a moment and Gov said, "Thanks, Doc—and Sam— It's gone now."

An attendant covered the unconscious subject up to its neck with a blanket and wheeled it away.

As we went back to the other room I had the most beautiful thought in the world, viz.: if *my* double was as sexless as Gov's, I didn't have a thing to worry about as far as Mae was concerned.

That wasn't quite accurate, of course. What it meant, if my promise was correct, was that I had one less thing to worry about. But it certainly was a very big relief to think that my little Mae was as safe in bed with the fake Sam Kent as she would be with a Teddy bear.

> The port is near, the bells I hear,
> the people all exulting.
> —Whitman

CHAPTER TWENTY-SEVEN
(AUG. 17, SUN.)

Gov's GUERRILLAS had spent the rest of Saturday and much of Sunday completing their examination of the android and making their plans for the rally. At least I assumed they were planning some kind of foray; no one told me very much and I had no idea what my role was to be, or if I was to be included at all.

The fat Sunday *Times,* the middleweight *Herald Tribune* and the radio filled me in on what was happening—or what appeared to be happening—in the outside world.

The Monolithian pretenders seemed to be solving a number of world problems.

The alien disguised as the President of the United Arab Republic announced a tentative settlement with Israel on the issue of the Palestine refugees.

The one posing as India's Prime Minister reported that he and Pakistan's leader had had a "meeting of the minds" on the explosive Kashmir question.

There was a curious dispatch from Taipei, full of Oriental undertones, which appeared to indicate that peace of a sort had been made between Formosa and the Communists in Peking.

There had been a tremendous kaffee-klatsch on the border of East and West Berlin and, while nothing was explicitly agreed to, the feeling was that the long division of Germany was coming to an end, in what a punning correspondent saw fit to refer to as "an arithmetical solution." The correspondent was vague on details but indubitably hopeful.

It was as if the fondest dreams of Moral Re-Armament were being realized. I looked for a happy communiqué from Mackinac Island on the subject, but there was nothing. I assumed the Buchmanites were sulking because the Monolithians had stolen their thunder.

I also looked in vain for a follow-up to "President Allison's" appeal to the nation to beware of imitations. The fact that there was no reference to it at all led me to think that the Monolithians had panicked only momentarily. It was obvious that they had known about the Allison underground. Their current silence on the matter gave me a small chill. It was as if the Monolithians were contemptuously tolerant of Gov's guerillas, seeing them as no threat whatever to the ultimate alien scheme.

I was mulling over this deflating thought when Timmie bustled in, saying, "Time to get ready, Mr. Kent."

He sat me down, wrapped a towel around my neck and proceeded to alter my appearance with grease pencil, nose putty and other backstage devices. It was the first inkling I had that I was to be a part of Operation Madison Square Garden.

Timmie backgrounded me and gave me my instructions as he worked deftly to make me look twice my age.

"That android, now. Doc didn't exactly take him apart, but he found out enough. He wasn't transmitting back to Monolithian headquarters, as we suspected, but he did have a kind of tape device inside his skull that recorded everything he saw and heard. In other words, he'd've had to get back to the aliens for his spying to've done them any good…

"We're all going to leave here at different times, so as not to be suspicious, and rendezvous at the Garden. You're to go in by the Press entrance on 49th Street. We've got some fake *Journal-American* credentials for you…"

There were a lot of cops at the 49th Street entrance. They were needed, because the street was packed solid with humanity and immobilized cars from Broadway to Eighth Avenue.

I shouldered my way through and flashed my police-press shield at a police sergeant, who waved me inside.

The first person I saw was Joy Linx. She was holding a sort of impromptu press briefing for a bunch of yelling reporters.

"Keep quiet a minute and I'll tell you," she was saying. "The President is going to come right up that aisle. You'll be as close to him as anybody. Then he goes up to the platform and Spookie Masters introduces him."

She was wearing a skirt and blouse and there were little beads of perspiration on her upper lip.

Somebody asked where Sam Kent was.

"I don't know," Joy said. "He was here a minute ago. He'll be back soon, I'm sure."

She glanced around, her eyes flitting over me without recognition.

People were jammed together on camp chairs all over the floor of the Garden. The speakers' stand was at the north end. There was red-white-and-blue bunting everywhere and banners reading "U.S. + M = Peace," "Give Common Sense a Try," and "Two Worlds Are Better Than One."

A band on the platform was in a segue from *God Bless America* to The *Battle Hymn of the Republic,* without losing a note, but it could barely be heard over the din of the 20,000 people who packed the Garden to the rafters.

I heard a yell from the street behind me. "He's coming!"

Other voices joined in: "It's Gov!" "Don't he look swell!" There was a chant: "We love Gov... We love Gov..."

True to Joy's word, Gov—that is, the Monolithian masquerading as the President—passed within a dozen feet of us on his way to the platform. He was accompanied by a dozen or more men who could have been the Secret Service or some of his fellow Monolithians.

The fake Gov smiled and waved to the masses of people in the Garden who were shouting themselves into a frenzy as section after section of them realized he was coming among them.

The band played *Hail to the Chief,* then *For He's a Jolly Good Fellow,* and finally *The Star-Spangled Banner.* It was quite impressive and I was patriotically moved despite my knowledge that it was all a fraud. I could imagine how the thousands in the Garden and the millions watching television felt. To them it must have been the culmination of mankind's yearning for respite from the decades of insecurity and fear of another global war, coupled with worship of that greatest of heroes, the man who had negotiated an interplanetary peace.

It was hot as hell and I longed to scratch my itching putty nose.

The Monolithian who was pretending to be the President seated himself behind a long table on the platform and Spookie Masters took over the microphone.

Spookie made a few jokes. Everything he said was greeted with laughter, cheers and applause. In that atmosphere he could have read a shopping list and won an ovation.

Finally he got down to business.

"Friends," he said, "—or maybe I should say fellow members of the interplanetary alliance—" (applause) "tonight we celebrate the passing of an old era and the birth of a new one. The change in which we participate tonight," he said solemnly, "and I choose my words carefully and with reverence and humility, is, I think, as historic as that which marked the division of the calendar from B.C. to A.D."

He paused, eyes cast down humbly, and a murmur went through the crowd. Somebody said, "Amen," and I half expected a Hallelujah or two, but Spookie hurried on before any revival meeting atmosphere had a chance to develop.

As he went on talking about interplanetary amity and the benefits to all mankind of this glorious turn in the history of the world, I saw Gov's guerrillas filtering through the aisles toward the platform. Some carried cameras, others had police-press shields paper-clipped to their lapels, and others merely wore ribbons printed with the word COMMITTEE. Nobody challenged any of them.

They got as close to the platform as they could.

Those with cameras brazened themselves closest and aimed their equipment directly at the fake President from less than a dozen feet away.

I knew what the equipment was, and I pushed closer myself to see whether it would work. It was the conscience gas I'd stolen from Ultra.

Gov's plan was a simple one—when the fake Gov got up to talk, dozens of cameras would record the scene. At the same time the conscience gas would spurt out of the guerrillas' cameras and smite the alien impostor.

The fake President would then go through the same mental turmoil that had assailed the dictator of El Spaniola. He would, in effect, become one with the thousands in the Garden and the millions on television who were about to be subjected to whatever nefarious fate the Monolithians had planned for them. The dichotomy of being simultaneously the victor and the victim would be too much for him. Then he would either confess everything or—if the Monolithians were actually a race with a common, interlocking intelligence, as some people suspected—he would make a decision in Earth's favor which would be binding on all the other aliens.

Either way, it would be interesting to watch.

Spookie was finishing his introduction. "And now, my dear friends everywhere, I give you the man you all know and love— the man who has had the courage and foresight to switch Earth's destiny in midstream from its course of destruction to its new and exciting path—your President and mine— Gouverneur—good old 'Gov'—Allison!"

The place went wild. Everybody stood up and yelled or cheered. Balloons of all colors with the words GOV and PEACE on them were released by the scores and floated up toward the roof. Confetti and streamers showered and spiraled down from the balconies. The band was playing fit to bust—but only visibly, not audibly, in the din.

The fake Gov stood there smiling, his arms out at his sides, waiting patiently to be heard.

I saw the quick bursts of flash bulbs, including ours, and watched the face of the alien masquerading as the President. There was no flicker of change in his expression of benevolence.

There was a scuffle somewhere on the floor. The center of the disturbance was where I had last seen the real Gov, disguised as a devoted follower of his impersonator. Four men had him by the arms and were moving him quickly and as inconspicuously as possible toward a curtained-off area near the platform. Then four men closed in on me. They took me by both arms, lifted me an inch off the floor and propelled me vertically in the same direction. "Hey," I began, but one of them said, "Come on, Kent. Don't make a commotion."

I didn't because I was well and truly outnumbered and, besides, each time I resisted they began to ruin my arms.

By the time I got to the curtained area the real Gov had been sat in a chair and stripped of his disguise by his Monolithian captors. All of our fellow conspirators were there, too, including the photographers whose cameras had been loaded with conscience gas instead of super-pan. I was crowded up against one of them and asked him, "Didn't you have a chance to shoot?"

"Sure I did. All of us did. But it didn't make a damn bit of difference. He's still out there lapping it up. Look at him."

I could see out to the platform, as from the wings of a stage. The noise of the crowd had diminished, but only slightly. The Monolithian duplicate of Gov still stood there. His smile seemed as genuine as ever and his conscience apparently didn't bother him in the least.

We must not gargle with euphoria.
—Charles de Gaulle

CHAPTER TWENTY-EIGHT
(AUG. 18, MON.)

GOV—THE REAL ONE—said to me, "It's as clear as that fake nose you were wearing last night that they sold you a pup, Sam."

I asked him what he meant.

"That so-called conscience gas we banked so much on. They must have engineered the whole thing, including your escape from Ultra."

Gov and I and the rest of his crew were at the penthouse office on Fifth Avenue.

The rally at Madison Square Garden had been a smashing success, as we'd been allowed to see, to our discomfiture, from the wings where we'd been herded after our capture.

We were now, on Monday morning, sitting or standing around in Addison Madison's office, wondering what was going to happen to us. The Monolithians had treated us gallantly so far, having put us up for the night at the Taft Hotel, guarded no more obtrusively than a bunch of suburban high-school seniors staying in town after the prom.

Now, at the Monolithian GHQ, though there was a constant flow of aliens in and out, none of them so far had had anything to say to us except busy good mornings. I didn't recognize any of them. Frij, alias Addison Madison, hadn't arrived yet, if he was due at all.

He had been very much in evidence at the Garden last night, public relationing in his most offensive manner, and I supposed he was still resting from his exertions which, Lord knew, had been a Monolithian triumph. The usually unimpressionable New York *Times* replated six times for it and gave it a three-line, eight-column banner head.

I had been trying to explain to Gov how he could tell one late city edition of the *Times* from another by the decreasing number of dots between the volume and number up under the left ear on page one, but all Gov had on his mind was the conscience-gas fiasco.

"Maybe they used their defense shield against it," Gov said. "Or maybe they're just naturally immune. But the best explanation is that they palmed off a phony on you when you swiped the stuff from Ultra. It was all just too pat to be real."

Addison Madison came in and said, "Oh, yeah, Mr. former President? Is that so?" He sounded as if he'd heard everything we'd said and when I asked him he had no qualms about admitting it.

"Let me tell you wise guys something," Addison Madison-Frij went on. "The conscience gas is the genuine article. It worked on General Rafael Domingo Sanchez of El Spaniola when we kept him from A-bombing your retrograde civilization and it also worked, believe it or not, on my colleague, the new President, at the Garden last night. So put that in your pipes and smoke it, Mr. Ex-President, and you, too, Mr. Ex-Hotshot Newspaperman."

"You're crazy," I said. "Let's assume for the sake of argument that it worked on Domingo Sanchez and that the Spaniola thing *wasn't* a hoax…"

"Your assumption would be correct," Frij said. "You don't know how irresponsible you Earthpeople are."

I let that go for the moment and said, "But your colleague, as you call him—the fake President Allison—was no more affected by the stuff in our phony cameras than the man in the moon."

"Ha ha," Frij said. "That shows how much you know. He was affected but it made no difference." He let that sink in for a while. "Do you want to know why?"

"Why?" Gov asked.

"Because," Frij said, "—now grasp this concept if you can— because my colleague, the new President, was sincere. His conscience was already clear."

Gov and I looked from him to each other. Much as we detested Frij, it began to dawn on us that he might be telling the truth.

"You mean," Gov said, "that it's true that you Monolithians have no purpose other than saving us from ourselves?"

"Precisely," Frij said. "You could not have put it more aptly."

"Then my story—the big expose Rod and I wrote on Ultra—was all wrong?"

"It couldn't have been more wrong," Frij said.

"And Domingo Sanchez wasn't your patsy?" I was slowly and reluctantly patching it together.

"You assumed that a minute ago," Frij said. "Now you believe it."

Gov, looking unutterably weary, said, "I'm afraid I believe it—and all that it implies. It means that Earth really had no choice whatever. The other Presidents and the Prime Ministers and I were forced to accept the Monolithians' terms to avert the Spaniolan threat—which I am now again convinced was no idle one. So we had to agree to the super-summit on Ultra, which, of course, set the stage for the substitution of Monolithian duplicates for Earth's leaders."

Gov smiled wanly and went on. "The fact that I sent a double of myself to Ultra only delayed matters slightly. You finally got me anyway."

Mox came in then. Like Frij before him, he obviously knew everything that had been said.

Mox, looking like a saint in his Monolithian robe, in contrast to Frij's flashy American clothes, said, "Frij, I think you've been out here too long. You've adopted not only the Earthman's protective coloration but some of his sadistic ways. Why haven't you told Mr. Allison why we wanted him?"

"I was coming to it," Frij said defensively.

"Go, Frij," Mox said. "I will tell him. Go back to Monolithia on the next lighter and re-enroll at the Foreign Service School for a refresher course in interplanetary relations.

Consider your punishment the fact that I have reprimanded you in public. Leave us now."

"Yes, Mox," Frij said humbly. He went out, and that was the last Earth saw of Addison Madison or anyone like him.

Mox smiled. "My apologies, gentlemen." He looked like dignity incarnate and I wondered suddenly if this were the mysterious "Mr. M.," the head Monolithian who had taken part in the conference on Ultra that decided Earth's fate. I halfway hoped so; he seemed so much the just, kindly, elder-statesman, father-image type who inspired trust and confidence.

Gov said, "Mr. Mox, I'm a tired old man, especially after last night. I'd appreciate it if you'd tell me what the hell's going on and, particularly, where I go from here. If I'm going to be led out and shot I'd just as soon get it over with, frankly, if it's all the same to you."

Mox looked shocked. "My dear sir," he said. "Nothing is further from our plans. All we want is for you to resume your rightful place in the White House, at the head of your government."

Gov exhaled a long sigh of relief.

Therefore he had no choice except to breathe in again—by which time Mox had crushed a tiny capsule in his palm and held it under Gov's nose.

> The score stands today: Strontium 90;
> Humanity 13.
> —James Thurber

CHAPTER TWENTY-NINE
(AUG. 19, TUES.)

TUESDAY WENT BY like a montage, or a series of fades and dissolves in a documentary movie.

Scene: The Fifth Avenue penthouse. *Mox's* (formerly Frij's) office. *Mox,* benevolent, wanting to be understood; *Sam Kent,* groping, wanting to be convinced.

Mox: There were several ways it might have been done. One requisite was a common denominator—something everybody uses, such as water. But water was not quick enough. Air is better.

SAM: You mean you contaminated the air?

Mox: Not contaminated, no. Diluted it, you might say. It started in El Spaniola, with Domingo Sanchez.

SAM: But you said—Frij said, up on Ultra—that it wasn't communicable.

Mox: Ah, but Frij lied to you. I don't know why; perhaps he had absorbed too many of Earth's ways. He was becoming dangerous. That's why I sent him home. Our conscience gas, as your press calls it, is transferable from person to person, and rapidly. Like your own oral polio vaccine, it is contagious on contact.

SAM (wordless): ! ! !

Mox: You need not look so horrified. Remember the greater good. Recall the game you've been playing with yourselves—a game where there is no winner. You had to be stopped because of the way the odds against survival were mounting. One of your more perceptive observers put it very well when he said the score stood Strontium 90, Humanity 13."

Gouverneur Allison, President of the United States, a good man basically and one who had long worried in his private soul, needed no more indoctrination than the whiff of conscience gas he'd been given by Mox to be convinced that the World's salvation lay not in the haphazard politics of Earthmen, but in the clear-seeing, galactic-minded altruism of Monolithian logic. He went back to Washington by Pennsylvania Railroad day coach, contaminating a few hundred people along the way, and when he got to the White House he signed an executive order as Commander-in-Chief directing that all American nuclear weapons be deactivated, transported expeditiously to the Challenger Deep, and sunk.

Immediately the four other atomic powers—Britain, the Soviet Union, France and El Spaniola—followed suit.

You could almost hear the collective sigh of relief that went up around the world.

Scene: Joy Linx's hotel room in Manhattan. *Joy Linx,* beautiful, hostile, in housecoat. *Sam Kent,* anxious, somewhat wild-eyed, truth-seeking.

JOY: All right, I guess. Come on in.

SAM: Listen, Joy, it's important.

JOY: It better be.

SAM: It's about Spookie Masters. How well do you know him? I mean really?

JOY: What kind of question is that?

SAM: I know it sounds crazy, Joy, but it's the key to the whole thing. Has he—did he ever—oh, God damn it, what I mean is, did he ever make love to you?

JOY (scornfully): I won't answer that stupid question. Did you think I would?

SAM: It isn't just me asking it, Joy. Honestly, you've got to realize how vital it is.

JOY: Look, Sam, my dear, sweet someone else's Sam: In a kind of crazy, hopeless way I once loved you. It was no good.

You know why. Mae, that's why. That lucky girl. So go away before you kill me any further, will you?

SAM (emotionally torn): Joy, Joy—how can I say I wish it were otherwise, when I both do and don't? Damn Mae (I don't mean that) and damn you—but particularly—damn me.

JOY (touched, quietly): Tell me what you want me to do.

SAM (with a sigh, then getting it over with): All right. When Spookie comes to see you, lead him on. Let him think you're crazy about him—as maybe you are.

JOY (looking at the floor, hands on Sam's chest): Maybe I am, in a second-best sort of way.

SAM (on brink of tears): Listen, my second-best darling… (a quick, antiseptic, apologetic kiss) what I have to know is— whether Spookie Masters is a Monolithian.

JOY (withdrawing): What!

SAM: That's the key to the whole thing. He could have come to Earth years ago as an advance agent for them—his early life has always been a mystery. His career took him all over the world. He knows everybody. Then he got himself to Ultra. Of course! *He* was the "Mr. M." who represented Monolithia at the super-summit.

JOY (coldly): Isn't that pretty far-fetched, Sam?

SAM: No. It fits perfectly. Then he arranged to get himself "captured" and thrown in with us so he could learn what we were up to. And I'll bet he engineered our "escape," too, and saw to it somehow that I stole that conscience gas. They knew I would lead them to the only holdout in their scheme—the real Gov—and that the gas would be the bait that put him in their trap at the Garden—where, you must admit, Spookie was very much the big wheel.

JOY (thoughtfully): Well, maybe. Tell me what you want me to do.

I'd told her, unable to look her in the eye, that I had to know whether Spookie Masters was a whole man, and therefore terrestrial, or a sexless creature like the android, and thus a

Monolithian. Joy had heard me out, saying nothing except with her contemptuous eyes, then showed me out.

Something puzzled me. I was feeling no pain. And yet I should have been, I reasoned, since I had been subjected to the C-gas at the same time Gov inhaled it and I was probing around in what must be considered an anti-Monolithian way.

I was also running around loose and doing a certain amount of independent thinking, which didn't seem to fit into the concept of a true Monolithian state whose subjects had been C-gassed into cooperating for the greater good.

True, I was on a loose rein. Mox had given me the day off, in effect, telling me to report to the White House in the morning. I supposed I'd find myself fired when I got there, since Gov's ex-guerrillas, including Josh Holcomb, his original press secretary, had all been C-gassed into conformity and my services would therefore be superfluous.

I decided to go back to the penthouse and have a heart-to-heart talk with Mox or one of his lieutenants.

Mox saw me himself. He must have had a million things to do, but he took the time to talk to me for more than an hour, answering every question I asked.

When I left his office I found Joy sitting at her desk, typing. She glanced at me and said, "Sit down, Sam. This is for you. I'll be through in a minute."

She rattled through another paragraph, then, after a look at me, typed one final line. With a pen she wrote two words. Joy sighed and said, "There—I've got that out of my system." She folded the single sheet of paper, sealed it in an envelope and handed it to me.

"Please go before you read it," she said.

Then she smiled, as if she were now at peace with me and the rest of the world.

"Joy—" I started to say.

"Just go—please," she said, and I went.

I read Joy's letter over a martini at a solitary table at the Brass Rail, then decided to have several more martinis and skip dinner altogether.

Joy's letter started: "Sam (not at all dear):" and went on to tell me quite explicitly that Spookie Masters—whom she called Robert, his real name—was male as male could be.

What she had said, actually, was: "He's as human as you are—if you are."

This was empirical knowledge, she said, not theory or hearsay. She had known this before today, she said, and hoped I was hurt by this fact as she had been hurt by me. She did not know whether Robert was an Earthman or a Monolithian, but this didn't matter to her. Her happiness was what mattered and it was obvious that I could only cause her pain.

"I've made my choice, Sam," she had written. "I had to choose between what I wanted and what I could get. There are times when the ideal is just too unattainable and when the second best becomes, in the long run, the best. Maybe this also has a universal application. I hope so."

The last line of her letter was: "One last thing, Sam—I hate you."

But she had edited this. One of her two handwritten words was her signature. The other, inserted in the last sentence above a caret, was "can't."

That had made her farewell read: "I can't hate you."

Over my third martini I thought I understood Joy's parting smile. Remembering it again, I could see the signs in her eyes. It wouldn't be long, I suspected, before I saw one of those headlines peculiar to the society pages of *The New York Times,* reading: TROTH PLIGHTED OF MRS. JOY LINX; MONOLITHIAN AIDE FIANCEE OF ENTERTAINMENT STAR.

I wished her joy and ordered a fourth martini.

Then I got up and telephoned Mae in Bethesda and told her I'd be home that night. Mox had told me, among other things, that my double wouldn't be there.

And now we all have a new King. I wish him
and you, his people, happiness and prosperity
with all my heart.
—Duke of Windsor

CHAPTER THIRTY
(AUG. 20, WED.)

IT'S DONE NOW. It's all over but the shouting, or maybe the weeping, depending on how you look at it.

Earth has been absorbed into the greater scheme of things.

There'd been a telephone call from the White House at 7 A.M., from Gov personally. There was no need for me to come in, he said. My job was intact but different. I wasn't the Presidential Press Secretary any more, but my new assignment was just as important—maybe more so. Mox, who came on the line on an extension, said the same, so I knew it was official.

I tried to explain it to Mae over breakfast.

"I'm the historian," I said. "That's what it's all about."

"Eat your eggs," she said. "They'll get cold." She had sprinkled them with Pep.

"My job is to write it just as it happened. The way I see it. No propaganda, no censorship."

"That's nice. You want your coffee now or later?"

"I can work at home if I want to. And they'll send out a secretary if I want somebody to type up notes or take dictation. Now, please."

"That's sweet of them," Mae said. She poured the coffee. "Maybe they'll send that nice Joy Linx."

I carefully broke a yolk and stirred Pep into it with my fork, giving it all my attention. I think Mae was serious. "I don't believe I'll need anybody," I said carefully.

"You need me." Mae was standing at the stove with her back to me, frying an egg for herself. She was wearing a sort of maternity middy blouse and skirt and looked very good. "Don't you?"

I got up and put my arms around her gently and kissed the back of her neck.

"You can hug us gently," she said.

I did. I thought I felt my son or daughter give a kick, not of protest, but just to let me know someone was there.

"Say it," Mae whispered.

"I love you and I need you," I said.

"Good." She gave her egg a poke and sighed as if in relief. "And I love you and need you. What I don't need is that crazy robot that's been hanging around pretending to be you."

"What!"

"He didn't fool me any—except at first."

"He didn't?"

"Oh, he's a very good imitation—as far as he goes. But he worked too hard at keeping me from finding out that he lacked a few male—or even human—necessities."

"You mean he didn't—uh, sleep with you?" I had to get it said, any old way.

"He certainly did *not*. Actually it was his own idea to sleep in the guest room. I'd have seen that he did anyway. But that wasn't the only thing. He never went to the bathroom."

"Well," I said.

"Oh, he'd go in and take a bath, but he never—how do they say it in hospitals?—he never *voided*."

"Oh? How do you know?"

"I listened at the door. There was never a sound till he flushed."

"Oh, Mae!" I said, not knowing whether to laugh or cry. "And I thought you were completely fooled, and that I had to stay away because if you saw two of us the shock would be too much for you. Why didn't you say something?"

"I figured it was important to you and your job, and maybe even the world. You usually have a good reason when you do something peculiar. Want some toast?"

"Yes, please—wait a minute. The toaster's broken."

'He fixed it. That's how I really knew he wasn't you. He went right ahead without a murmur and repaired half a dozen things you've been putting off ever since we were married, practically. He fixed the stuck zippers and my sewing machine and that lamp with the short in it and the switch on the vacuum cleaner. That wasn't my fumble-fingered old Sam."

All that was a long time ago. It's been only a little more than two years, but it seems like ancient history now.

A lot has happened since. It's all been fully recounted and interpreted in the press and magazines, so I'll just hit the highlights.

A year ago all the nuclear weapons in the world were deactivated and sunk in a remote corner of the Pacific. The scientists who were working on bigger and worse ones were transferred to peaceful research.

Six months ago the Moon was colonized by a six-man international expedition, whose names are Underwood, Chihho, Cohen, Raswaplindi, Buragin and Thorwald, and their wives.

Five months ago the cure for cancer was announced. They'd solved the riddle of muscular dystrophy, Parkinson's disease and arthritis before that.

Last week the people of Mississippi elected a Negro governor.

For more than a year a few million people who had been on the brink of starvation have had enough to eat—and the U.S. government is saving a few billion dollars a year by not paying storage charges on surplus grain. (Our farmers have never had it so good, either, and the take-home pay of factory workers has doubled in the past year.)

Income taxes are now so low that there's a bill in Congress to abolish them altogether.

Someone said this should be called the Half-Century of the Common-Sense Man.

Earth's population explosion has been controlled to the satisfaction of both the Catholic Church and the economists and

Antarctica is becoming a populated continent. It's actually warm under the ice where the mining and living is going on.

You've read about it. There's something new and wonderful almost every day.

Mae says I have to put in some personal stuff, like the name of our son (Kevin) and the fact that Mr. and Mrs. Robert (Spookie) Masters came to the christening as godparents and how we have dinner with Spookie and Joy, or vice versa, every Friday night when he's not making a movie or being on TV.

I'd better make it clear that Spookie's not a Monolithian, though he was among the first to dig them, as he puts it with no shame. And he's recently become the father of a beautiful little girl. So much for my doubts about his sex life.

World Wide has been de-nationalized and Ian McEachern went back and Stew Macon and all the rest are still with it. There's a good job there for me, too, when I finish my book.

Eurydice Playfair got awfully bored with the Monolithians when the initial glamour wore off for her. For a while there was talk about her marrying one of them (they're all quite male, except for their robot-androids, which have been deactivated), but she broke that off and went to the Caribbean and, I heard, opened up a fashion house, or some kind of house.

President Gouverneur Allison backed his Vice-President for the top spot on the ticket and he was duly nominated at the convention. The other party nominated its man but there was little to choose between. Both espoused the good and peaceful life our country has come to know and, though there was nothing explicit, there were pro-Monolithian overtones to each candidate's campaign.

It didn't matter which won, as had been proven in the elections of other countries. All on Earth, I thought sometimes, were contented cows—happy, unambitious and no longer obsessed by the fear of an annihilating war.

Crime vanished as the effects of the conscience gas spread inexorably around the world. This gave a boost to the common welfare—the billions of dollars, pounds, francs, marks, rubles and drachmas which had been illegally drained off almost as a matter of course showed up where they belonged: in the pockets of honest people.

Despite my vow to retain my objectivity I've had to fight to avoid succumbing to the pervading conviction that all's well with the world. But maybe I should stop fighting. "Monolithian" has practically become a lower-case word—like humanitarian or altruistic or philanthropic. It almost never connotes anything alien.

It's as if the Monolithian philosophy has been thoroughly absorbed into our culture, while the aliens themselves have retreated into the background, content to keep a paternalistic eye on us.

Oh, they're still with us, physically, but I think they're getting ready to go. They're a bit wistful about it, not wanting to be forgotten. They've apparently absorbed that Earthly trait of vanity, which may be one reason—a minor one, I'm sure—for my project under what has become the Monolithian Foundation.

I'm compiling the history of their visit under a grant probably more generous than any writer ever received. I'm writing it exactly as I see it, as I told Mae, without guidance, restraint or censorship. I think they'd like it finished before they go back, so they can take a copy with them, but there's no deadline. It shouldn't take me more than another six months, now that I've finished the day-by-day account of the first month of their visit.

There's some talk of publishing these working notes immediately in a popular version, perhaps under the title *30-Day Wonder,* or *The Peaceful Invasion.* A doctor friend of mine has suggested *The Febrifuge,* which my Little Oxford tells me is a medicine to reduce fever, and, though I like the thought it expresses, it doesn't have much zing.

As I wind it up I really don't see how I can come to any valid conclusion. I've been too close to everything.

It's all down on paper now, except for the footnotes and the documents and the index.

I've said all I can and I still don't know what's right, except for me and my family, who have never been so happy or secure.

But is this enough? Frankly, it's enough for me. For now. Twenty years from now I hope to ask my son the same question. And I hope he'll know what I'm talking about.

THE END

If you've enjoyed this book, you will not want to miss these terrific titles...

ARMCHAIR SCI-FI & HORROR DOUBLE NOVELS, $12.95 each

D-61 **THE MAN WHO STOPPED AT NOTHING** by Paul W. Fairman
TEN FROM INFINITY by Ivar Jorgensen

D-62 **WORLDS WITHIN** by Rog Phillips
THE SLAVE by C.M. Kornbluth

D-63 **SECRET OF THE BLACK PLANET** by Milton Lesser
THE OUTCASTS OF SOLAR III by Emmett McDowell

D-64 **WEB OF THE WORLDS** by Harry Harrison and Katherine MacLean
RULE GOLDEN by Damon Knight

D-65 **TEN TO THE STARS** by Raymond Z. Gallun
THE CONQUERORS by David H. Keller, M. D.

D-66 **THE HORDE FROM INFINITY** by Dwight V. Swain
THE DAY THE EARTH FROZE by Gerald Hatch

D-67 **THE WAR OF THE WORLDS** by H. G. Wells
THE TIME MACHINE by H. G. Wells

D-68 **STARCOMBERS** by Edmond Hamilton
THE YEAR WHEN STARDUST FELL by Raymond F. Jones

D-69 **HOCUS-POCUS UNIVERSE** by Jack Williamson
QUEEN OF THE PANTHER WORLD by Berkeley Livingston

D-70 **BATTERING RAMS OF SPACE** by Don Wilcox
DOOMSDAY WING by George H. Smith

ARMCHAIR SCIENCE FICTION CLASSICS, $12.95 each

C-19 **EMPIRE OF JEGGA**
by David V. Reed

C-20 **THE TOMORROW PEOPLE**
by Judith Merril

C-21 **THE MAN FROM YESTERDAY**
by Howard Browne as by Lee Francis

C-22 **THE TIME TRADERS**
by Andre Norton

C-23 **ISLANDS OF SPACE**
by John W. Campbell

C-24 **THE GALAXY PRIMES**
by E. E. "Doc" Smith

If you've enjoyed this book, you will not want to miss these terrific titles...

ARMCHAIR SCI-FI & HORROR DOUBLE NOVELS, $12.95 each

D-71   **THE DEEP END** by Gregory Luce
TO WATCH BY NIGHT by Robert Moore Williams

D-72   **SWORDSMAN OF LOST TERRA** by Poul Anderson
PLANET OF GHOSTS by David V. Reed

D-73   **MOON OF BATTLE** by J. J. Allerton
THE MUTANT WEAPON by Murray Leinster

D-74   **OLD SPACEMEN NEVER DIE!** John Jakes
RETURN TO EARTH by Bryan Berry

D-75   **THE THING FROM UNDERNEATH** by Milton Lesser
OPERATION INTERSTELLAR by George O. Smith

D-76   **THE BURNING WORLD** by Algis Budrys
FOREVER IS TOO LONG by Chester S. Geier

D-77   **THE COSMIC JUNKMAN** by Rog Phillips
THE ULTIMATE WEAPON by John W. Campbell

D-78   **THE TIES OF EARTH** by James H. Schmitz
CUE FOR QUIET by Thomas L. Sherred

D-79   **SECRET OF THE MARTIANS** by Paul W. Fairman
THE VARIABLE MAN by Philip K. Dick

D-80   **THE GREEN GIRL** by Jack Williamson
THE ROBOT PERIL by Don Wilcox

ARMCHAIR SCIENCE FICTION CLASSICS, $12.95 each

C-25   **THE STAR KINGS**
by Edmond Hamilton

C-26   **NOT IN SOLITUDE**
by Kenneth Gantz

C-32   **PROMETHEUS II**
by S. J. Byrne

ARMCHAIR SCI-FI & HORROR GEMS SERIES, $12.95 each

G-7   **SCIENCE FICTION GEMS, Vol. Four**
Jack Sharkey and others

G-8   **HORROR GEMS, Vol. Four**
Seabury Quinn and others

If you've enjoyed this book, you will not want to miss these terrific titles…

ARMCHAIR SCI-FI & HORROR DOUBLE NOVELS, $12.95 each

D-81   **THE LAST PLEA** by Robert Bloch
          THE STATUS CIVILIZATION by Robert Sheckley

D-82   **WOMAN FROM ANOTHER PLANET** by Frank Belknap Long
          HOMECALLING by Judith Merril

D-83   **WHEN TWO WORLDS MEET** by Robert Moore Williams
          THE MAN WHO HAD NO BRAINS by Jeff Sutton

D-84   **THE SPECTRE OF SUICIDE SWAMP** by E. K. Jarvis
          IT'S MAGIC, YOU DOPE! by Jack Sharkey

D-85   **THE STARSHIP FROM SIRIUS** by Rog Phillips
          FINAL WEAPON by Everett Cole

D-86   **TREASURE ON THUNDER MOON** by Edmond Hamilton
          TRAIL OF THE ASTROGAR by Henry Haase

D-87   **THE VENUS ENIGMA** by Joe Gibson
          THE WOMAN IN SKIN 13 by Paul W. Fairman

D-88   **THE MAD ROBOT** by William P. McGivern
          THE RUNNING MAN by J. Holly Hunter

D-89   **VENGEANCE OF KYVOR** by Randall Garrett
          AT THE EARTH'S CORE by Edgar Rice Burroughs

D-90   **DWELLERS OF THE DEEP** by Don Wilcox
          NIGHT OF THE LONG KNIVES by Fritz Leiber

ARMCHAIR SCIENCE FICTION CLASSICS, $12.95 each

C-28   **THE MAN FROM TOMORROW**
          by Stanton A. Coblentz

C-29   **THE GREEN MAN OF GRAYPEC**
          by Festus Pragnell

C-30   **THE SHAVER MYSTERY, Book Four**
          by Richard S. Shaver

ARMCHAIR MASTERS OF SCIENCE FICTION SERIES, $16.95 each

MS-7   **MASTERS OF SCIENCE FICTION AND FANTASY, Vol. Seven**
          Lester del Rey, "The Band Played On" and other tales

MS-8   **MASTERS OF SCIENCE FICTION, Vol. Eight**
          Milton Lesser, "'A' as in Android" and other tales

If you've enjoyed this book, you will not want to miss these terrific titles…

Made in the USA
San Bernardino, CA
02 April 2018